Jarrid glanced up at Becky. "Do you want me to go on?"

Her legs suddenly felt weak. "Sure, why wouldn't I?"

Jarrid read on. "I think about your lips against mine...your hands caressing my body. I need you, Jarrid. I need you so much." He slowly slipped the letter back into the envelope. "Do you really mean that, Becky?"

"Wh-why else would I have written it?"

She prayed he didn't hear the trembling in her voice. Still, the words her twin had written to bring Jarrid and Becky together were *exactly* how she felt about him.

Jarrid's eyes searched hers. "Are you sure you want to start something between us again?"

Start? She wanted to *begin,* continue and stay with him forever, but would he still want her when he learned she wasn't his old girlfriend?

Dear Reader,

Hello! For the past few months I'm sure you've noticed the new (but probably familiar) name at the bottom of this letter. I was previously the senior editor of the Silhouette Romance line, and now, as senior editor of Silhouette Desire, I'm thrilled to bring you six sensuous, deeply emotional Silhouette Desire novels every month by some of the bestselling—and most beloved— authors in the genre.

January begins with *The Cowboy Steals a Lady,* January's MAN OF THE MONTH title and the latest book in bestselling author Anne McAllister's CODE OF THE WEST series. You should see the look on Shane Nichols's handsome face when he realizes he's stolen the wrong woman…especially when she doesn't mind being stolen or trapped with Mr. January one bit….

Wife for a Night by Carol Grace is a sexy tale of a woman who'd been too young for her handsome groom-to-be years ago, but is all grown up now…. And in Raye Morgan's *The Hand-Picked Bride,* what's a man to do when he craves the lady he'd hand-picked to be his brother's bride?

Plus, we have *Tall, Dark and Temporary* by Susan Connell, the latest in THE GIRLS MOST LIKELY TO… miniseries; *The Love Twin* by ultrasensuous writer Patty Salier; and Judith McWilliams's *The Boss, the Beauty and the Bargain.* All as irresistible as they sound!

I hope you enjoy January's selections, and here's to a very happy New Year (with promises of many more Silhouette Desire novels you won't want to miss)!

Regards,

Melissa Senate

Melissa Senate
Senior Editor

Please address questions and book requests to:
Silhouette Reader Service
U.S.: 3010 Walden Ave., P.O. Box 1325, Buffalo, NY 14269
Canadian: P.O. Box 609, Fort Erie, Ont. L2A 5X3

PATTY SALIER

THE LOVE TWIN

SILHOUETTE *Desire*

Published by Silhouette Books

America's Publisher of Contemporary Romance

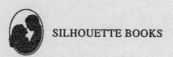

SILHOUETTE BOOKS

ISBN 0-373-76121-X

THE LOVE TWIN

Copyright © 1998 by Patricia Bury Salier

This edition published by arrangement with Harlequin Books S.A.

® and TM are trademarks of Harlequin Books S.A., used under license.
Trademarks indicated with ® are registered in the United States Patent
and Trademark Office, the Canadian Trade Marks Office and in other
countries.

Printed in U.S.A.

Books by Patty Salier

Silhouette Desire

The Sex Test #1032
The Honeymoon House #1091
The Love Twin #1121

PATTY SALIER

Born and raised in Gravesend, Brooklyn, in New York, Patty credits her mother for her keen logic and her father for her curious, creative mind. She has been a published writer for many years. To Patty, her wonderful husband and two great children are everything she could want in life. "I've got so much to be thankful for."

To Lucia Macro—
a most encouraging, inspiring and very creative editor

One

Early morning, at her gym in Los Angeles, Becky Lawson was doing floor exercises when she suddenly met the eyes of a striking man in the distance.

He was looking at Becky like he knew her. For a moment she felt like she knew him, too. Yet she was sure she'd never met him before.

As the music pulsed, Becky quickly glanced behind her at the other leotard-clad women working out. She was positive that a ruggedly handsome guy like him couldn't be staring at her. But when she looked back through the glass wall of the exercise room, his eyes were still on her.

He was standing near the men's locker-room door, beside the indoor pool, with a black gym bag on his left shoulder. She noticed his curly brown hair, sparkling brown eyes, denim shorts and green T-shirt that hugged the solid muscles of his chest.

Becky could barely hear the aerobics instructor calling

out the exercise count. His sexy gaze made her almost forget she was at the gym.

The warm expression in his eyes caused an immediate electrical charge through her entire body. Her skin heated up. She couldn't concentrate on her bun pumps.

Who was he? Why was he looking at her when the room was filled with more beautiful, exciting women? And why did she feel like she wanted to rush out of the room and go straight into his powerful arms?

"Becky, your cheeks are flaming red!" Becky heard Charlotte Swanson say as she hurried in to take a spot on the floor mat beside her. "I hope these exercises aren't *that* strenuous."

Becky wanted to die of embarrassment. His sensual gaze had turned her on so much that even Charlotte had noticed. She forced her attention off him, but her skin felt feverish at the thought that he was still looking at her.

She tried to focus on talking to Charlotte as she exercised. Charlotte, who was in her mid-forties, owned a successful advertising agency in Los Angeles. The agency where Becky hoped and prayed she could get a great job for her identical twin sister, Pam. Becky had been separated from her identical twin since birth, and for twenty-four long years, she didn't even know she had a twin. More than anything, she wanted her sister to move from New York to live with her and become a family in Los Angeles.

"Do you think you might have a job opening for Pam?" Becky nervously asked.

"Becky, does your sister want one or two file cabinets in her office?" Charlotte replied.

Becky suddenly felt like she was dreaming. "Oh, Charlotte!" she burst out, excitedly. "Do you really have a job for Pam?"

"One of my account executives will be leaving the

agency in four weeks," Charlotte continued as she exercised. "I'll know more details when I return to the office."

Becky's mind was spinning with joy. "I appreciate your help so much! If there's anything I can do for you—like give you two free months of hairstyling at your home—let me know."

"Becky, I'm the one who owes you," Charlotte responded. "You make me look beautiful every week when I visit you at the Nouveau Hair Salon, even on days when I feel awful. Can you drop by my office in the next hour or so to discuss the job for your sister?"

Becky couldn't contain her glee. "I'll be there!" Becky wasn't going to let anything keep her and her identical twin apart ever again.

In the midst of her exhilaration, her gaze drifted back to the pool area. Her heart pumped wildly as she spotted him again. He was smiling and warmly shaking hands with Joe Demme, the aquatics director. As he talked, he glanced over at her. His luminous eyes lingered on her for a long moment.

She suddenly became aware that her legs were spread wide apart in the bun squeeze, and she was rhythmically lifting her body up and down in an erotic motion on the floor. Her nipples hardened under her leotard. A tingly, pleasurable sensation she'd never felt before radiated between her thighs.

Stunned and embarrassed by her sensual response, Becky looked away from him and jumped up to the standing position for the next exercise. Her cheeks flamed. The skin under her neck-high leotard burned with perspiration.

As she raised her arms to the music beat, she nervously glanced around the exercise room to see if anyone had noticed how turned on she was. What was going on with her? It wasn't like her to be fantasizing about a man she'd never seen before in her entire life.

* * *

Near the indoor pool area, Jarrid Browning was unable to take his eyes off her. *It couldn't be Becky!* he silently told himself. Had she recognized him, too?

His heart hammered against his ribs. He hadn't seen her in seven years. Memories of being close to her flashed through his head. Memories he'd long forgotten.

He watched her black leotard-clad body move smoothly, sensually, to the beat of the music. His gaze lingered on her abundant breasts as they bounced under the tight leotard.

For a moment Jarrid forgot what had happened between them seven years ago. He forgot that he was completely over her. And he felt a tug at his heart for Becky that was stronger than he remembered.

Becky barely recalled cooling down with the class. Her hand was trembling as she grabbed her towel. Unable to stop herself, she glanced at the pool area, remembering those warm brown eyes of his linked to hers for those few eternal moments. But now he was gone.

She glanced around the gym searching for him, and then she stopped, stunned at herself. She'd never chased after a man before. She'd always been shy with men, even with her ex-boyfriend, Darryl Burton. She often wondered if that was one of the qualities about her that had caused Darryl to turn away from her.

Realizing she would be late for her appointment with Charlotte, Becky hurried toward the women's locker room near the pool area to take a quick shower.

Rushing alongside the deep end of the pool, she mentally flashed on the sparkling eyes of the guy who'd been staring at her and wondered who he was. She was so caught up in her fantasy about him that she barely heard someone call out to watch for the slippery pool tiles.

Suddenly Becky's feet slipped out from under her, and

she plunged into the cool deep pool water. She felt herself sink, sink, sink under the depths of the chlorine blue.

Deafening, gurgly, bubbling sounds filled her ears. A raging fear of drowning paralyzed her. Panicking, she struggled to hold her breath, but her mouth burst open. Water gushed into her lungs.

All at once, a pair of strong hands grabbed her waist and pulled her up, up, until loud voices hit her ears.

There was blackness all around as she felt her motionless body being gently laid down on wet tiles. She felt her leotard being torn from around her neck to try to help her breathe. Fingers were on her throat and there was a hand on her chest feeling for her heartbeat. Then warm lips covered her mouth.

Fresh oxygen filled her lungs. Her eyes slowly opened. His mouth was pressed against hers, breathing air into her. His strong hand lay gently on her chest, just above her breasts, making sure her heart was working.

It was *him!*

In her barely conscious state, Becky felt her body burn fire hot from his lips and touch.

Just then she heard the relieved voice of the aquatics director saying, "Jarrid, her eyes are opening! She's breathing!"

Jarrid. Jarrid. His name ran hypnotically through her mind over and over.

When she felt Jarrid's mouth release from hers and his warm hand lift off her chest, she wanted to cry out for more of his electrical touch.

"Becky, are you okay?" Jarrid's deep voice whispered her name with great concern, like he knew her, like she was someone who meant everything to him.

Before she could speak, she started coughing up water. She felt Jarrid's firm hands steady on her back to help her sit up. As Becky tried to rise to her feet, a rush of dizziness filled her head. Jarrid grabbed her by the shoulders and pulled her close so she could lean on him.

"I've got you, Becky," he whispered, as though he really cared.

She realized that her cheek was against his bare, muscled chest. She could feel the wiry brown hairs on his skin near her lips, evoking a powerful erotic reaction in her.

Embarrassed, Becky quickly sobered up. Her equilibrium returned. She gently slipped out of his strong arms, feeling her face burning with shame. She prayed he didn't notice how turned on she was in his presence.

She saw Joe Demme pat Jarrid on the back. "I knew my swimming workouts would get you in shape, Browning. Now you're saving lives."

Jarrid Browning's eyes met hers. A tingly sensation raced through her veins.

"It was definitely my pleasure," he said, as though he was talking only to her.

The circle of people around her dispersed, but Jarrid didn't budge. Several adult swimmers dived into the pool for the start of the swim workout.

"Thanks for pulling me out of the pool," Becky said, her cheeks burning from being close to him. "I've got a terrifying fear of the water. "

"I know, Becky," Jarrid said. "You almost drowned when you were two years old."

Becky stared at him. She *did* almost drown in a swimming pool when she was two years old.

"How do you know my name?" she asked in an unsteady voice. "And how do you know I almost drowned as a child?"

Jarrid was a bit out of breath from his mouth-to-mouth with Becky. His heart was pumping wildly from being near her again. Her captivating emerald eyes looked up at him. Her wet strawberry blond hair fell down her ivory shoulders. Water droplets were on her eyebrows. Her cheeks looked soft and pink. Her lips were fuller than he remembered.

Jarrid felt an intensity of emotion he'd never experienced with her before. He still couldn't believe that she was standing right in front of him.

"Becky, come on," he said. "You told me, remember?"

"I did not," she responded.

"How can you say that?" he asked, a bit taken aback. "Sure, it's been seven years since we were together in New York, but I can still remember every single detail about you."

"New York?" she repeated, incredulously. "I've never been to New York."

She was unbelievable. "Geez, Becky. I know you like to kid around, but—"

"I'm *not* joking."

He tilted his head, staring at her. "Remember the first time I met you?" he asked. "You pretended you didn't understand one syllable of English. For days, you had me believing you had just stepped off the plane from Paris."

She put her hand on her hip. "I'm sorry, but that wasn't me."

He couldn't help but smile. "Really? Are you married? Is that why you're putting on this act?"

"I don't have a husband," she insisted. "And I'm not pretending. You're mistaking me for somebody else."

"Who?" he demanded. "Your twin sister?"

Her eyes lit up. "That's right!" she quickly said. "You're thinking I'm Pam, my identical twin sister. She lives in New York and—"

"Becky, come off it," Jarrid cut in. "I know you're adopted and don't have a twin sister named Pam. I also remember you told me that you were searching for your birth mother and wanted to change your last name to your birth name. So why are treating me like I'm a stranger? I saw you staring at me when you were doing aerobics a little while ago.''

Her cheeks turned apple red. "I—I thought I knew you, but I don't.''

Jarrid felt a sudden sadness rush through him. "Sure, Becky, I understand. A goodbye is a goodbye, isn't it?'' He glanced up at the wall clock. "I'm late for my swim workout.''

He forced himself to dive into the pool. She didn't want to be with him, and that was it. Unable to deal with his disappointment, he forcefully swam across the water, trying to wipe out the denial in her eyes.

Confused and unsure of what had just happened, Becky rushed into the locker room. She fumbled with her combination lock, slipped off her leotard and hurried into the open shower. Her friend Sherry, who was also a hairstylist at the Nouveau Hair Salon in Beverly Hills, had finished working out on the weight machines and was drying off from her shower.

As Becky turned on the cool water, her naked body still sizzled from Jarrid Browning's survival touch. She noticed that her bare nipples were protruding with arousal. Embarrassed, she quickly turned so Sherry wouldn't notice.

"Becky, are you all right?'' Sherry asked with concern.

"I—I'm fine, thanks, Sherry.'' She admired Sherry and looked up to her. Sherry was in her late thirties, very happily married and had two kids who were in high school.

"Becky, I noticed you were in *very* sturdy hands at the pool,'' Sherry commented.

Becky nervously rubbed faster as she shampooed her hair. "Jarrid Browning definitely knows his life-saving techniques.'' She didn't dare tell Sherry how sexually excited she felt with his hands so close to her breasts and his mouth covering hers.

"You can't fool me, Becky," Sherry said with a know-ing twinkle in her eyes. "I saw the steam rising between you and him. Maybe he'll ask you out."

Becky bit her bottom lip. "I don't think so."

Deep down, she knew the stark truth about herself. She wasn't sexy enough for any man to want to be with forever. Her ex-boyfriend, Darryl, had made that crystal clear to her.

"I bet he asks for your phone number," Sherry said, grabbing her soap, shampoo and towel to leave. "I saw the way he looked at you. When my husband looked at me when we first met, I *knew* I was going to marry him. Now I've had seventeen wonderful years with him to prove I was right." Then she hurried to her locker.

Becky turned off the shower water. She knew Sherry was bull's-eye about her attraction to Jarrid. From the moment she saw him, she knew she could instantly fall in love with him.

Yet, she knew that a raw, masculine guy like Jarrid could never be interested in a woman like her. Besides, she wasn't even the Becky he thought she was!

In the parking lot outside the gym, Jarrid anxiously leaned against his silver van, still holding his gym bag. His insides were churning like the pool water had during his workout.

He knew he needed to get to work at the small home entertainment store he owned in Santa Monica, but instead, he glanced through the windowed pool area at the closed women's locker-room door, waiting for Becky. She was still inside taking a shower, probably washing away any memory she ever had of him.

Jarrid kicked his work boot into a pothole, thinking about Becky—his old sweetheart—the girl he had wanted to marry.

He painfully remembered his last heart-wrenching night

with her. It was the evening of Becky's high school senior prom. Becky had looked like a princess in her turquoise gown. She was a bold, vivacious eighteen-year-old, while he was a naive, crazy-in-love, twenty-one-year-old audio and video technician.

Her prom night also marked their two-year anniversary of going steady. He had excitedly hidden a purple velvet box containing a round miniature-diamond engagement ring in his black tuxedo jacket. He couldn't wait to surprise her.

In the back seat of the chauffeured, black limousine Jarrid had rented for the night, he got up the nerve to hand her the velvet box. He anxiously waited for the yes that would light up his life.

As Becky stared at the sparkling ring, her bottom lip had trembled. When she closed the box without putting the diamond on her finger, Jarrid had known her answer.

In a rush of words, Becky had told him that she was eager to start college and begin a baking-fresh new life. She yearned to be free to adventure with new souls.

Jarrid didn't recall slipping the velvet box back into his tuxedo pocket, or even her prom. He knew why she'd turned him down.

He blamed himself. He was the one who'd pushed her into going steady. He was the one who'd wanted to see her every single weekend. He'd fooled himself into believing that she was in love with him as much as he was with her.

That night was the last time he saw Becky. Until seven years later—carrying her out of the gym pool in Los Angeles.

Jarrid's heart suddenly quickened when the women's locker room door opened. He held his breath as he waited for Becky to appear. Instead, a woman carrying a red gym bag hurried out.

What're you doing to yourself, Browning? he mentally scolded. *You got over Becky a long time ago.*

And he did. When his heart had eventually healed, he told himself that he could live without a woman's love. And whenever he had felt lonely, he reminded himself of how hurt he'd gotten when he let love rule his life.

He had moved to Los Angeles and taken a job as an electronics technician for a chain store. He had worked hard and finally saved enough money to start his own small home entertainment store selling carousel CD players, surround sound speakers, four-channel power amplifiers, laser disc players and digital satellite dishes.

However, Jarrid had bigger dreams. He wanted to custom design and install home theater systems and corporate video and audio systems. Then he could someday open a much larger home entertainment store showcasing his designs and hire more employees. To do that, he first needed to attract customers who could afford to contract him to design custom systems. And so far, he hadn't even come close to his goal.

Yet, no matter how hard Jarrid worked at expanding his business, he still secretly yearned to find the woman of his heart. And now Becky had reappeared.

Just moments ago, when he tore down Becky's high-top leotard neckline to help her breath, his eyes caught the swell of her breasts above her exercise bra. He felt the impulse to cup her firm mounds in his hands.

And when his mouth covered hers to blow air into her lungs, why did he allow himself to taste the honey sweetness of her?

Jarrid knew why. He'd momentarily fantasized that Becky had changed. That she would want to be with him forever the way he'd wanted her seven years ago.

Jarrid yanked open his van door and hurled his gym bag

into the front seat. *Who're you kidding? Wasn't it obvious that Becky was trying to brush you off?*

Come on—she never lived in New York? She had an identical twin sister? *Face it, Browning. Becky still doesn't want to become a serious part of your life and never will.*

Just then, Jarrid saw the door swing open again. His heart pumped faster as Becky stepped out and walked toward the parking lot.

She was wearing a calf-length flowered skirt and loose white blouse. She had a touch of powder pink lipstick on her rosebud lips, and her strawberry blond hair bounced as she walked.

As she passed him, he smelled sweet roses and felt the impulse to reach out and stop her. He yearned to know who she was now. As he watched her, he saw her face flush from his blatant stare. Then she quickly got into her car and drove off.

Jarrid realized that maybe he didn't know Becky after all. He remembered how sensually she had dressed in high school with form-fitting skirts and hugging sweater tops. He had never once seen her wearing a flowing skirt and button-down blouse.

A ray of hope filled his heart. Maybe he should pursue her, get to know her on a new level.

Jarrid squeezed the chrome door handle of his van, wondering if he could open his heart to her again, knowing she again might shatter it to pieces.

He climbed into his van and drove to his store, needing to bury himself in his business, needing to forget that the sight of Becky made him want her all over again.

Becky zipped along palm-tree-lined Venice Boulevard in her red VW Rabbit heading towards Charlotte's office to find out the details of that advertising job for Pam. She had a couple of hours before she had to be at the hair salon for her first appointment.

However, she could barely think about work or her sister's new job. Jarrid Browning filled her every thought.

Becky desperately needed to talk to her twin. She had to find out who Jarrid was to her. Instead of going straight to Charlotte's, she made a U-turn and headed toward her Mar Vista apartment.

In her living room, Becky first dialed Charlotte's office to tell her that she would be a few minutes late. When she got Charlotte on the line, the executive had said she'd call her right back.

Becky hoped that Charlotte didn't think she was being flaky by not going straight to her office and prayed she hadn't ruined Pam's chances of getting that new job.

Becky then anxiously called her sister's office in New York where she was an account executive at an advertising agency.

"Pam Lawson's office," the secretary said over the phone.

As always, Becky was thrilled when Pam's personal secretary answered her call. She was so proud of her twin's career success. Her secretary asked if Becky could wait a few moments for Pam to get off the other line.

As Becky nervously waited, she remembered the first moment she'd found out that she had an identical twin sister.

One year ago she had opened the door to her apartment, and Pam had been standing there. Stunned, Becky had felt as if she was looking into a full-length mirror.

"Becky, it's me," Pam said, her green eyes welling up with tears. "I'm your twin sister!"

A sob had caught in Becky's throat as she hugged her twin, holding her and not wanting to ever let go.

Becky had stayed up all night talking with Pam. Her

sister remained at her apartment for two straight weeks until she had to return to her job in New York.

With disbelief, Becky listened as Pam told her that she had found their birth mother right before she died of cancer. She learned that she and Pam got separated at birth because their real mother wasn't married and had decided to give them up for adoption to two different couples.

Their birth mother had never told either adoptive couple about the existence of the other identical twin. She was afraid that no one would want to adopt two baby girls together or want to keep them apart if they knew.

Becky was astonished to discover that her identical twin had, like her, also been adopted by an elderly couple who had passed away. Her sister had also been named Becky—after their adoptive grandmothers who coincidentally had the same first name—and she was also afraid of the dark and of the water, because she had almost drowned as a little girl.

Within a week, Becky and her identical twin had immediately changed their different adoptive last names to their birth mother's surname, Lawson. And her sister had changed her first name to Pam, their birth mother's first name.

"Beck, I was just thinking about you!" Pam's voice traveled across the fiber optic line from the Big Apple, breaking into Becky's warm memories. "My bones have been tingling for the last two hours feeling like something wonderful has happened to you!"

"I think I found a great job for you," Becky said, explaining about Charlotte's possible L.A. job for her.

"Wow!" her sister responded. "You mean we'll be together soon? When do I start, Beck?"

"Maybe in four weeks." Becky replied. "I'll let you know when you need to give your notice at your New York job."

"I can't wait!" her twin added and then stopped. "There's something else, isn't there? I can feel it three-thousand miles away."

Becky sat down to steady herself. "Pam, do you remember Jarrid Browning?"

"Jarrid?" her sister repeated, incredulously. "You saw him today?"

Saw him? She was in his muscled arms! "He goes to the same gym as I do."

"I can't believe it!" Pam said, excited. "Jarrid was my very first love in high school. How did he look? What did you think of him?"

The words flew out of Becky's mouth before she knew what hit her. "He's sensitive, courageous, caring." She abruptly stopped. What was she saying? How could she tell Pam that Jarrid made her body so hot she needed an ice bath to cool down?

"You liked Jarrid a lot, didn't you?" Pam asked, reading her mind. "I can hear it in your voice."

Becky's cheeks heated up. "He's okay, I guess."

"Beck, for once, will you admit your true feelings?" Pam said, almost like she *wanted* her to like Jarrid. "Sometimes I worry that you're so closed up because of what happened with your old boyfriend, Darryl, that you wouldn't see the man of your dreams even if he kissed you on the lips."

He did almost kiss me, she wanted to say about Jarrid, but she couldn't. Not until she knew for sure that Pam no longer had feelings for him.

"Jarrid thought I was you," Becky hurried on, telling her sister about how he saved her from drowning in the pool. "He even knew about my fear of the water because you and I almost drowned as kids."

Her sister's voice rose an octave. "Did you play along

with him? Did you tell him you *were* me to see his reaction?''

"Of course not!''

"Why not? You could've gotten to know him.''

All of Becky's insecurities about being with a man again rose up in her. "I told Jarrid I was your twin sister, but he didn't believe me.''

She felt so nervous that she got up from the chair and walked over to the window facing the jacaranda trees lining her street.

"This is wild!'' her twin exclaimed. "Of course he didn't believe you, because I was always joking and playing tricks on him.'' Then Pam's voice lowered. "Is Jarrid still angry with me for splitting up with him?''

That's why he looked hurt when she insisted she didn't know him. He thought Pam was rejecting him again.

"Pam, why did you break up with him?'' she asked.

"I never meant to hurt him,'' her sister explained, telling her about Jarrid's marriage proposal. "Jarrid wanted a wife, but I was too young to get married. I needed to explore who I was. But now, Beck, I wonder if I made a terrible mistake.''

"What do you mean?'' Becky wanted her sister to find happiness with a man, because Pam couldn't seem to settle down with one man in her life. Yet she secretly wished that man wouldn't be Jarrid Browning!

"Beck, maybe I was dumb back then,'' Pam hurried on. "I've dated so many guys since Jarrid, but I've never met a man as special as him. Do you think he really is the one for me?''

Becky felt momentarily speechless. "Well, sure, I mean, he might be, I guess.'' Deep down, she wanted to hear her sister say that she had no feelings at all for Jarrid.

"Beck, I know this sounds totally insane,'' Pam rushed on. "But could you keep Jarrid thinking you're me?''

Becky couldn't breathe. "What?"

"I don't want to lose him again," her sister quickly explained. "I can't prove to Jarrid that I still care about him when I'm so far away. I need him to see how sorry I am for tearing us apart. Beck, can you do that for me?"

Her throat felt dry. "I—I can't. I'm not you, Pam."

"Exactly," Pam hurried on. "I'm so bold and impulsive. That's what made me lose Jarrid in the first place. But you're sweet and sincere, Beck. You can open his heart to me again. Please, Beck, play like you're me—just until I move to Los Angeles for that job you'll be getting for me."

Becky's mind was whirling. She *wanted* to say yes so she could have an excuse to see Jarrid again. Yet the whole idea was plain crazy.

"Pam, I don't know anything about you and Jarrid," she stammered. "I don't think I can pretend—"

"I'll special deliver you my high school diary," her twin cut in. "I wrote down every detail of my relationship with him."

"What will happen when Jarrid finds out you've fooled him?" she worriedly asked. "It won't be fair to him, Pam."

"Jarrid knows I'm a joker card," her sister explained. "And he'll doubly appreciate all I did to get him back. Plus, you'll get to spend time with a wonderful man after depriving yourself of male company for so long. Come on, Beck, will you do this super favor for me?"

Just then, Becky's call waiting clicked on the phone. She felt a moment of torturous relief.

"Pam, hold on a sec. It's Charlotte about your new job." She quickly switched to the waiting call. "Charlotte, I can be at your office at whatever time is best for—"

"Becky," Jarrid's deep voice resonated in her ear, "I hope you don't mind my calling. I got your number from the membership list at the gym."

"Jarrid—" Becky's heart started wildly pumping. "Could you hold on a moment? I'm on another call."

"If this is a bad time—"

"Oh, no, you're perfect, I mean, it's okay," she stammered, her heart fluttering. "I'll be right back."

Becky anxiously switched to her sister. "Pam, it's Jarrid. What am I going to tell him?"

"Beck, here's your opportunity!" her sister said, excitedly. "Will you treat him special for me? Ask him to lunch. That'll make him feel great."

"I can't!" Becky blurted. "I've never asked a man to lunch before."

"Jarrid won't believe you're me if you play Ms. Shy and Reserved," Pam said. "Let go of your silly inhibitions. Be spontaneous for once in your life."

"Pam, I don't know if I can—"

"I gotta go," Pam quickly cut in. "I love you, sis! Good luck!" Then she hung up.

Becky's hand was sweating as she held the phone receiver, knowing Jarrid was waiting for her on the other line. She felt weak at the knees, exhilarated and terrified at the same time.

Get close to Jarrid? That was her ultimate fantasy the very second she met him.

Her heart was thumping as she put a trembly finger on the button that would connect her with Jarrid. She couldn't do it! Pam had to understand. It wasn't in her to pursue a man, especially someone as incredible as Jarrid Browning!

Two

In the small office at the back of his store in Santa Monica, Jarrid anxiously squeezed the phone in his hand. He was so hyped up he couldn't even think straight. He wondered why Becky was taking so long to come back to his call. Was she thinking of excuses to hang up on him?

Stop being paranoid, he told himself. He was sure she sounded excited when he first called. Or was he just imagining it to convince himself that he could steal back into her heart?

He didn't even know why he was calling. He had an appointment at a customer's house in Beverly Hills to deliver a sixty-inch, high-tech television screen. His technician, Pete, was waiting for him in the van out front. But he couldn't go until he talked to Becky.

"Jarrid, I'm sorry I took so long," her soft voice suddenly whispered in his ear.

He swallowed. "Becky, I know you don't want to talk to me."

"Yes, I do," she quickly cut in.

He held his breath. "Then why did you pretend you didn't know me at the pool?"

"Because my mind was all foggy and cluttered," she rushed on. "Yours would be, too, if your nose and throat were clogged with chlorine."

He had to smile. "Maybe I *was* a bit overly sensitive." He instinctively put the receiver closer to his lips. "Wouldn't you still be sensitive if you were on my end the night of your prom?"

He felt her hesitate. "Jarrid, I was really immature then," she began. "I didn't know what I was saying."

Jarrid's hopes rose. "What do you mean, Becky?"

Becky felt a rush of excitement hearing Jarrid's deep, masculine voice so close to her ear. She nervously glanced at the framed photograph of her and Pam arm in arm hanging on her living room wall. *Pam, help!* she silently begged.

"Jarrid, I wasn't very good at communicating my feelings back then," she disclosed, trying to think of what her sister might say. "I was too abrupt and insensitive. I should've told you I was too young to get married. I should've been more gentle with you."

Jarrid was silent for a long moment, and she wondered if she'd said the wrong thing. She didn't want to mess it up for her sister. Becky knew she shouldn't have agreed to this and planned to call Pam back and tell her she couldn't pretend to be her a moment longer just as soon as she hung up with Jarrid.

"I'm confused, Becky," Jarrid admitted. "Half of me wants to see you again. But the other half—"

"Do you think you might be able to ignore that second half?"

His voice was almost a whisper. "Do you really want me to?"

She could almost feel his warm breath on her cheek. A tingle of pleasure cascaded from her breasts down to her toes. Her heart fluttered wishing it was *her* he was talking about wanting to see. But remembering her sister's love for him, she ignored her own response to him.

"Jarrid, can't we start over? I mean, seven years have gone by, and we're both so different now."

"I want to, Becky, but I've got to be honest with you." She heard him hesitate. "My sister-in-law, Marie, is setting up a date for me with her friend."

Becky suddenly panicked. She had to do something fast before Pam lost Jarrid a second time. Should she ask him to lunch like Pam wanted?

"Jarrid, would you like to, I mean, I was wondering if—"

"Becky," Jarrid interrupted as a male voice called him in the background. "I'm late for a business appointment. Can we continue this conversation?"

"Yes, definitely! Where? When?" she blurted.

What was happening to her? She was never that bold.

"I could drop by where you work late tomorrow afternoon," he said.

"Oh, no, not there." She didn't dare take that chance. What if someone at the salon said something that might let him know that she wasn't the same Becky? "How about at your job?"

"Great!" Jarrid said, excitedly. "I'll show you my home entertainment store."

"You own a store?" she asked, surprised and impressed at the same time.

"Yeah, it's kind of small, but it's mine."

She was so nervous and excited that she could barely remember writing down the Santa Monica address of his store before she hung up the phone. She knew she should immediately call Pam to tell her that she couldn't pretend to be her with Jarrid.

Yet she couldn't back out on her sister now, not when Jarrid was about to meet another woman and Pam wasn't in Los Angeles to win him back.

Why deny it? She couldn't wait to be with him again. She couldn't wait to see his store. She couldn't wait to continue their talk. She couldn't wait—

The sound of the phone ringing interrupted her wayward thoughts. She quickly came back to reality when she heard Charlotte's voice on the line.

"Becky, how about dropping by my office tomorrow after lunch instead of today?" Charlotte suggested.

"Sure, Charlotte. I'll be there about 1:30. Thanks so much."

Suddenly, a rush of anxiety filled Becky's body. Her twin might be moving to Los Angeles in a few short weeks. So why didn't she feel as joyous about it as she did before?

Because of Jarrid Browning, that's why!

Feeling tense, and still having a little time before her first appointment at the salon, Becky grabbed her keys and went out for a walk to quell the uncontrolled feelings she was having about Jarrid.

Under the flower-scented jacaranda trees, Becky followed the hilly sidewalk, breathing in the ocean-filled Mar Vista air. She had to concentrate on getting Jarrid back for Pam. She had to forget her own yearning for him.

As she turned the corner on busy Centinela Avenue, her heartbeat sped up when she spotted a curly brown-haired, muscular guy in shorts jogging across the street. For a second he looked just like Jarrid.

Her skin heated up with desire just thinking about him. She quickly turned away, silently scolding herself for wanting the man her sister was still in love with. She hurried back to her apartment to call Pam in New York. She had to keep her sister's interest in mind, not her own.

She dialed Pam's office number desperately needing tips on how to win Jarrid's heart back for her twin. But it was lunchtime in New York, and she got Pam's voice mail. So Becky left a message asking her sister's advice on how she should act with Jarrid when she saw him again.

As she hung up, Becky was determined about one thing. She was going to get Jarrid back for her twin. However, as she grabbed her car keys to drive to the salon, she was a bundle of raw nerves, trying to figure out how she was going to silence her own major attraction to Jarrid Browning.

"Uncle Jarrid, sit next to me!" his nine-year-old niece, Lizzy, squealed as she pulled him to the dinner table at his brother Kenny's house in West Los Angeles that evening.

Jarrid gently kissed her hand. "Lizzy Browning, I'd be honored to be your dinner partner." In a princelike manner, he pulled out a chair for her.

How many times had Jarrid wished he had a daughter just like Lizzy and a beautiful wife like his brother had.

"Uncle Jarrid, I heard my mom's gonna set you up in a few days with her girlfriend," Lizzy whispered in his ear. "I've never met her, but don't worry, I'll let you know straight-out if she's right for you."

"I'm counting on your opinion," Jarrid said, warmly hugging his niece, but his insides were churning.

Before Becky reappeared, he had been looking forward to meeting Marie's friend, who was recently divorced and searching for a relationship like he was. But now, he felt uneasy about it.

All because of Becky.

"Jarrid, how's your business going?" Kenny asked as

he helped his wife set plates of meat loaf, mashed potatoes, cooked baby carrots and salad onto the dinner table.

"I'm still looking for customers who'll hire me to design video and audio systems for them," Jarrid replied, relieved to get his mind momentarily off his emotional turmoil about Becky. "Know of any, Kenny?"

"Wish I did," his brother replied. "I'd send them straight your way."

"Yeah," Jarrid said, thoughtfully. "I just need to find a way to get my name out there. Then I'll be able to open the larger store I keep dreaming about."

Kenny high-fived him. "I know you're gonna make it big, bro!"

"By the way, Jarrid," Marie began as she passed him the meat loaf. "I heard you're swimming at the gym now. Getting in shape for a new relationship?"

His brother winked at him. "I bet he's met a couple of cute single women there, right, Jarrid?"

"Ken, stop it!" Marie said. "I don't want your brother meeting another woman."

Jarrid avoided Marie's eyes. "Don't worry, Marie, I haven't met anyone new at the gym." He immediately piled meat loaf onto his plate, not wanting his sister-in-law to know about his confused feelings about Becky and spoil her dating plans.

"Good," Marie said. "Because I already told my friend, Leah, about you. She's dying to meet you."

"Same here," Jarrid responded, trying to summon his original enthusiasm.

Kenny eyed him for a long moment. Jarrid got the distinct feeling that his brother sensed something was up but was going to keep quiet so as not to ruin things for his wife.

"How do you want to meet Leah?" Marie pursued. "A

blind date with just the two of you? A family barbecue here?''

''Family, definitely, barbecue, here with all of you,'' Jarrid rushed in a jumble of words. With Becky haunting his mind, he wanted to meet Marie's friend in a friendly, platonic atmosphere.

Once again, Jarrid felt Kenny's eyes on him. His brother was eight years older and twenty years wiser. Even as a kid, Jarrid could never put one past his big brother.

''Terrific!'' Marie said, excitedly. ''How about next Saturday?''

''Fine with me,'' Jarrid replied, his stomach in one tight knot.

He was relieved when dinner ended. Lizzy talked him into a game of Monopoly, and he lost all his play money and properties when he landed on her hotels on Park Place and Boardwalk.

But later, while Marie tucked in Lizzy for the night, Kenny cornered him while he played his brother's new CD-ROM computer game.

''Come clean, little brother,'' Kenny said, egging him on. ''You *did* meet a lady at the gym, didn't you?''

Jarrid could feel the meat loaf grumbling in his intestines. ''An old girlfriend.''

Kenny's eyes widened. ''You only had *one* old girlfriend, Jarrid. Wasn't she the high school girl who burned you?''

Jarrid anxiously jerked the computer joy stick and missed the game target on the screen. ''Yeah. Becky.''

''I never met her, did I?'' Kenny went on. ''I think Marie, Lizzy, and I were living in Chicago then. But I remember when you came to visit us, how broken up you were.''

I'm still in pieces! Jarrid wanted to yell out but didn't. He had to find a place in himself that was emotionally neutral about her.

"Kenny, you've got to promise not to tell Marie," he said. "I don't want to spoil her plans. I'll work this out. It won't affect meeting her friend."

Kenny's eyebrow lifted. "You're still hooked on Becky, aren't you?"

Jarrid quickly got up from the computer. "I don't know, Kenny, I don't know."

Kenny put a brotherly arm around his shoulders. "I know you well, Jarrid," he began. "Ever since Mom and Pop died in that car accident when you were seventeen, you've been looking for a girl to love. Don't worry. It's gonna happen for you. Your future wife is out there. Just trust the process."

Jarrid nodded, trying to absorb his married brother's wisdom. He knew that seven years ago he'd held on too tightly to Becky because of his desperate need to love and be loved. He had emotionally paid for his overwhelming need when she eventually broke free of him. He didn't want to make that same mistake twice.

"Hey, Jarrid, how about a quick one-on-one basketball game before you go?" his brother asked.

"Sure," he replied, hoping the game would help get Becky out of his mind.

As Jarrid shot for the hoop, Becky's strawberry hair and green eyes flashed through his head. Suddenly, he made a clear basket. A slow grin crossed his face. He couldn't help but wonder if that perfect shot was an omen of good luck for him and her.

At the Nouveau Hair Salon in Beverly Hills, Becky quickly stuffed her hair dryer, hair spray, gel and scissors into her bag. She was already a few minutes late for her appointment at the Beverly Hills home of Mrs. Gwen Fuller, who preferred having her hair styled in privacy.

Becky didn't mind doing house calls. Most of her clients

at the salon were upscale, wealthy women who had busy schedules to keep.

As Becky packed her bag, she made sure she also had her swimsuit along. Mrs. Fuller always insisted that Becky swim in her pool. However, when she learned of Becky's fear of drowning, Mrs. Fuller made sure that Becky relaxed in her Jacuzzi after Becky did her hair. Becky couldn't refuse because she knew Mrs. Fuller was a widow who enjoyed sharing the lavish home she lived in by herself.

Becky anxiously glanced at the clock on the salon wall. She couldn't even think straight, knowing she would be seeing Jarrid at his store in several hours. First, she had to go to her meeting with Charlotte about her sister's job.

She still hadn't talked to Pam about how she should act with him to be convincing. Her twin had left a message on her home answering machine saying she was overloaded with work and couldn't call back until later.

However, her sister said she'd sent her diary special delivery, and she'd come up with other super-cool ways to help her get over her shyness with Jarrid.

Becky was so blind with worry that she accidentally knocked over her bag. Her favorite pink satin blouse fell onto the linoleum salon floor—the pretty blouse she wanted to change into before seeing Jarrid.

Sherry quickly picked up her satin blouse and smiled. "Are you going out with Jarrid Browning?"

"Yes, I mean, no. He wants to show me his store." She wished she could tell Sherry about Pam's scheme, but she couldn't break her sister's confidence.

"How wonderful!" Sherry said. "He's opening his life to you. That's a true sign that he cares."

"Do you really think so?" Becky asked, momentarily forgetting she was going to see Jarrid because of her sister.

"Absolutely," her friend said supportively. "When a

man wants to show off where he works, you can be sure he's *very* interested in you."

Becky's stomach was jumping with butterflies as she gathered up her bag and hurried to her car in the parking structure. She felt so jittery and unsure about herself that she wondered if she should call him from Mrs. Fuller's and postpone seeing him until she got more advice from Pam.

With her mind in a frenzy about what she should do, she drove as if on automatic pilot along Sunset Boulevard and turned onto a street lined with vast estates and palm trees. The gates were open to Mrs. Fuller's property, and she saw the gardener putting a lawnmower into his pickup truck, getting ready to leave.

As she parked her car, she was in such a rush that she barely saw a van parked at the far end of the driveway. She grabbed her hair supply bag and ran through the side entrance which took her straight to Mrs. Fuller's private bathroom.

As Jarrid adjusted the wires behind the projection television screen in Mrs. Fuller's spacious living room, he felt excited about Becky's meeting him at his store.

He couldn't wait to show her the business he'd started. He wanted her to see the work space he was renting and meet Pete, his competent and loyal technician.

He planned to show her the high-tech audio/visual equipment he was selling. But most of all, he wanted to show her the sketches of home theater systems he'd designed in the hopes of getting future customers interested in the work he really wanted to do.

As he fine-tuned the picture on the television screen, his shoulders and back suddenly started to ache with tension. Doubts about re-entering Becky's life rose up in him with tornado force. Would he start wanting her so much again that he would set himself up for another rejection from her?

"Jarrid, could you do me a favor?" Mrs. Fuller said from behind him. She was wearing a hair salon smock and had rollers in her hair.

"What would you like me to do for you, Mrs. Fuller?" he asked, packing up his tools.

He had met Mrs. Fuller a few years ago when he worked for another store. She'd remained a loyal customer when he got his own place of business and called him periodically to upgrade her equipment so that she could entertain her married children and grandchildren when they visited her.

"Could you check out the television sets in the three bedrooms in the guest house?" she asked. "The remote doesn't work on any of them."

"Sure, no problem," he gladly replied, thankful to have her as a steady customer.

"By the way," she added. "After you finish, feel free to take a swim in the pool before you go. My housekeeper will leave swim trunks for you in the guest house."

He was about to politely decline since Pete would be waiting for him at the store, but he didn't want to hurt Mrs. Fuller's feelings. Besides, a few laps in the pool would be just what he needed to relax his tense body.

"I might take you up on it, Mrs. Fuller," he replied with a smile.

"Terrific," she said. "My hairdresser is finishing my hair. Then I'll be leaving, so I'll say goodbye for now."

As Jarrid headed outside toward the guest house, which was a short distance from the main house, he noticed the shimmering blue water of the oblong swimming pool and the swirling foam of the hot tub.

He could feel the tension in his shoulder and back muscles already easing knowing he'd be taking a short swim and maybe even hop into the Jacuzzi.

He wanted to feel comfortable when he was with Becky.

He wanted to show her that he didn't need her love as desperately as he did when he first knew her. He wanted to start a gradual friendship with her. Nothing too heavy. In that way he wouldn't set himself up to be hurt again.

Becky spread the floral-scented gel into Mrs. Fuller's sleekly cut short hair. Mrs. Fuller mentioned something about a technician working in the guest house, but she was too wound up to completely listen.

She had made her decision. She was going to call Jarrid after she took a Jacuzzi and postpone stopping by his store, at least until she received her sister's diary.

"Do you like this new style, Mrs. Fuller?" Becky asked, hoping to please her one hundred and fifty percent. She handed Mrs. Fuller a mirror and twirled the seat around giving her a back view of her hairstyle.

"Becky, it's beautiful!" Mrs. Fuller said, happily. "You make me look so young." She paid her generously for the cut and added a twenty-dollar tip.

"Oh, no, Mrs. Fuller," Becky began. "You've paid me way too much already."

Mrs. Fuller gently pushed the money back into Becky's hand. "Now put on your swimsuit and jump into the hot tub. You look tense." Mrs. Fuller picked up her purse. "I'll see you next week."

Becky knew Mrs. Fuller was right. She was wired to the max about calling Jarrid. Maybe a quick Jacuzzi soak would settle her down a bit and then she'd know what to say to him.

Becky slipped on her powder blue, one-piece spandex swimsuit in Mrs. Fuller's bathroom and then grabbed a towel. As she walked out of the back patio glass doors, Becky suddenly froze.

There was Jarrid emerging from Mrs. Fuller's pool!

Her breath caught at how handsome he was. He was

wearing grass green swim trunks, and his skin glistened from the dripping water and sunlight. As he wiped down his muscled arms and legs with a towel, she gazed at his wide shoulders and broad bare chest.

Her eyes traveled down to his ample manhood pressing against the thin wet fabric of his swim trunks. Her skin burned hot. She'd never blatantly stared at a man with such sultry thoughts in her entire life!

Just as Jarrid stepped into the Jacuzzi, he turned, and his eyes met hers.

"Becky!" A gleaming smile flashed on his face. "Are *you* Mrs. Fuller's hair stylist?"

She quickly nodded. "I work at the Nouveau Hair Salon in Beverly Hills," she replied, trying to keep a calm voice when she was dying inside seeing him again. "Are you the technician she was talking about?"

"Yeah!" he replied, his eyes twinkling as though he was thrilled to see her. "I just installed a new television set for her. She talked me into taking a swim. You, too, huh?"

"Just a dip in the Jacuzzi." She became very aware of standing half-naked in front of him.

"Come on and join me," he offered.

She caught his gaze slowly travel down her swimsuited body. His eyes lingered on her breasts. She felt her nipples growing hard from his visual caress.

Becky hesitated. She couldn't get into that small Jacuzzi with Jarrid, not when he was bringing out sensual feelings she'd never felt before, not even when she was with her ex-boyfriend, Darryl.

I'm here with Jarrid for Pam! she silently reminded herself. Knowing how forward Pam was, she was sure that her twin would want her to take a Jacuzzi with him. She had to act a little bolder like her sister to be convincing.

Becky slowly walked toward the bubbling hot tub, trying

to contain her excitement at being with him, trying not to feel her undeniable magnetic attraction to him.

As the warm water swirled around him, Jarrid watched Becky walk toward him. The elastic fabric of her blue swimsuit hugged the roundness of her abundant breasts. Her shapely bare legs looked soft and golden in the sun. He immediately fantasized about touching the warm skin of her inner thighs.

Just then Jarrid noticed Becky nervously clasping and unclasping her hands as she reached the hot tub, as though she didn't know what to say or do. He was momentarily surprised. The Becky he used to know was impetuous and impulsive. She said and did whatever came to her head, unaware of what anyone thought about her.

Steam from the Jacuzzi swirled between them. He held out his hand, and she hesitantly slipped her fingers through his. He guided her into the white foam. She sat down across from him, looking a bit unsure. He wanted to draw her into his arms, but he held back.

His gaze locked on her shimmering eyes. Her cheeks were flushed. Her lips powder pink.

"You look beautiful, Becky, more beautiful than I remember." The words rushed out before he could control himself. "I've been thinking about you all morning."

Her face reddened. "Me, too, about you."

"You have?" he asked, wanting very badly to believe he still had a chance with her.

"Oh, yes," she responded.

Her rosebud lips parted a little. Her sweetness, her vulnerability, all of it made him ache to kiss her.

"What have you been thinking?" he asked.

"How excited I am at seeing you again," she said in a shaky voice.

"Not as excited as I feel."

"Wanna bet?" she added in a teasing tone.

His gaze traveled down her swimsuit. Her nipples protruded through the wet material as though she was naked in front of him.

He swallowed, wanting to touch her, caress her. He could feel his maleness responding under the swirling water.

Slow down, Browning, slow down! he told himself.

But he didn't listen. Being near her brought out a longing within him that was more powerful than he'd ever felt for her. He impulsively leaned closer to her and gently touched her warm cheek with his palm.

"It's crazy, Becky, but I almost feel like we're meeting for the very first time."

"We are," she replied and then quickly added, "I mean, in seven years, we've both changed a lot."

"You definitely have." He traced her full lips with his thumb. "You're an incredible woman now."

Then he trailed his finger down her neck to the soft cleavage of her breasts, across the swollen hills, with his eyes steady on hers. He felt her tremble under his touch, as if he'd never caressed her before.

As his mouth closed over hers, he heard a voice call out, "Mr. Browning, you have a phone call."

He turned and saw the housekeeper standing at the sliding glass door. "Okay, thanks," he responded. "I'll be right there."

When he turned back to Becky, she was already out of the Jacuzzi with a towel wrapped around her body.

"Jarrid, I need to get back to the salon," she said, her voice quivering a little.

"Will I see you later at my store?"

"I—I was wondering if we could do it another day," she hesitantly asked. "I'm running late, and I might have to squeeze a couple of appointments in tonight."

Disappointment filled him. "Sure, I understand. We'll do

it later.'' But deep down, he felt her drawing away from him.

As she hurried back to the main building, Jarrid felt the impulse to call her back. He needed to tell her that he hadn't meant to move so quickly. He didn't mean to put any pressure on her. All he'd wanted was to get close to her.

Becky raced into Mrs. Fuller's bathroom. Her skin was still flaming from Jarrid's touch. She didn't dare go to his store now. She'd gotten so turned on by him that she would've blended into his kiss with no holding back if the housekeeper hadn't shown up.

Under the cool shower, Becky could still feel Jarrid's warm finger caressing the tops of her breasts and his mouth touching hers. She ached to feel his strong hands cupping her breasts, pressing his palms against her nipples.

She abruptly turned off the shower water. *What am I thinking? I'm with Jarrid for Pam, not myself!*

Jarrid didn't say *she* was beautiful. He wasn't touching *her* lips. He wasn't about to kiss *her*. In his mind, he was with Pam.

As Becky frantically dried herself, she glanced at her watch. Her appointment with Charlotte! She'd totally forgotten about the meeting about her sister's job. She was so caught up in Jarrid that nothing existed for her except him.

How could she have put her own attraction to Jarrid ahead of getting her sister that L.A. job?

Becky yanked on her clothes feeling upset with herself. As she hurried out of the house, she glanced down the driveway looking for Jarrid's van, but it was gone. She should've felt relieved, but instead, she missed seeing him.

Her head started to ache as she quickly got into her car. She prayed that Charlotte would tell her Pam's job would be available sooner than she thought. She had to get her sister moved to Los Angeles right away. Because she couldn't be in Jarrid's presence without thinking about her own need for him!

Jarrid made a pit stop at his West Los Angeles apartment for a quick bite to eat before responding to the phone call he had received at Mrs. Fuller's house from Pete. Pete told him that he had heard from a friend that Lyle Industries in Santa Monica wanted remote video monitors installed in each of their ten executive offices for video-conferencing purposes.

Jarrid wanted to go over to Lyle Industries in person and convince Mr. Lyle that he was the man to design their video system.

He grabbed a cold piece of leftover chicken from the refrigerator. He tried to concentrate on what he would say to Mr. Lyle, but his mind was whirling with conflicts about Becky.

In the Jacuzzi, Becky was so open to him. Her eyes held a warm caring that momentarily melted away the long-ago memories of her refusing to marry him. She looked at him like he was a new man to her, like she was getting to know him all over again.

Yet she'd acted so cool to him afterward. She wouldn't even go to his store like they'd planned.

Jarrid hurled the bare chicken bone into the trash can. *Move on with your life,* he silently told himself.

In a few days he would be meeting Marie's friend. She could be the woman who would accept him completely. The woman who would want to share her heart and soul with him.

Yet why did the idea of dating a woman other than Becky feel so wrong to him? If Becky wasn't going to get seriously involved with him again, why didn't he feel enthusiastic about Saturday night at Kenny's?

Jarrid grabbed his van keys so he wouldn't delay getting to Lyle Industries to discuss his video conferencing ideas.

Just as he opened the door to leave, he found a delivery man dressed in brown shorts and brown shirt standing there ready to ring his doorbell. He was holding a special delivery letter and a clipboard for his signature.

Jarrid quickly signed the receipt form and hurried to his van with the letter in his hand.

At a red light, he glanced at the envelope to see who it was from. There was no return address. He drove into the subterranean parking structure of the office building in Santa Monica, turning into the first empty parking spot he saw.

Jarrid couldn't stop himself from taking a few short moments to open the envelope. He immediately spotted the typewritten name at the bottom of the letter. It was from Becky.

His heart hammered against his ribs. He wondered if she was going to tell him that she didn't want to see him anymore. He focused on the typed words.

Dear Jarrid:
I guess I've gotten a bit shy over the years. It's so hard for me to say how I feel about you when I'm with you. Will you forgive me for hurting you on my prom night? I think about you a lot. I see your face in my mind when I'm working. I see your sexy eyes. And when I'm lying in bed at night—

"Hey, buddy, you're parked in a reserved spot!" Jarrid heard the parking attendant call out.

"Sorry!" he quickly yelled back, his stomach churning over Becky's revealing letter.

Jarrid quickly shoved Becky's red-hot letter back into the envelope, slipped it in his pocket and drove to the spot the attendant pointed to. She was bold in her letter, like the Becky he knew. Yet, in person, she presented a softer, shier side that appealed to him even more.

When Jarrid entered the gray-carpeted, lamplit reception area, he was told to wait a few minutes. Becky's inviting words filled his head. Having a couple of minutes, he took out her letter and quickly read the rest.

Becky couldn't relax sitting in the plush floral chair in Charlotte Swanson's advertising office in Beverly Hills. Somehow, she had to get her sister to L.A. sooner than Charlotte had in mind for that job. She couldn't go on another second pretending to be her twin when she wanted so badly to be with Jarrid herself.

She had stopped by her apartment before going to Charlotte's office to see if Pam's diary had been delivered, but there was no mail waiting for her. Her message machine was blinking with a call, but she was a couple of minutes late for her appointment with Charlotte and didn't take the time to listen to it.

She saw Charlotte glance up from her three-way conference call on her videophone and motion that she would be with her in a moment.

Becky politely nodded, feeling the tension growing inside of her. She picked up the framed family photograph on her friend's desktop of Charlotte, her husband and three children.

She admired the closeness between Charlotte and her husband. For a split second she imagined her and Jarrid in the photo as husband and wife with his protective arm around her waist, gazing at her with those brown eyes of his filled with more love than she could ever dream of.

"Becky, about your sister," Charlotte began, flicking off the videophone screen.

"Yes, of course, my sister."

Becky quickly set the photograph back on the desk. Every time her thoughts drifted to Jarrid, she forgot about Pam. Her fantasies about him were growing steadily out of control.

"I hope you don't mind, Becky," Charlotte said, "but I called your sister in New York early this morning. I offered her a very desirable salary and benefits package."

"Oh, Charlotte, thank you so much," she said. "How soon can Pam come to Los Angeles?"

"Actually, there might be a slight delay."

"A delay?" Becky repeated uneasily.

"The account exec who is leaving the position your sister will fill told me that she is still negotiating a contract with her new employer," Charlotte explained. "She asked to remain at her job for a while longer until the signed document is in her hand."

Becky anxiously straightened in the chair. "How long will that take?"

"We're looking at possibly another four to five weeks, because her new employer is out of town."

Four to five more weeks with Jarrid!

Becky's forehead started to pound. She could barely hear Charlotte say that she had already informed Pam of the delay, and her sister seemed fine about it.

Charlotte's videophone buzzed, and she glanced at the caller I.D. number. "Unfortunately, Becky, I'm going to be on this call for a while. I'll let you and Pam know the second my employee gives me her final date."

Becky stood up, fidgeting with her purse, her mind in major discord. "Charlotte, thanks a trillion for your help." She warmly shook her hand.

As Becky drove back to the hair salon, she barely noticed driving past the glitzy department stores and the prestigious international bank buildings on Wilshire Boulevard.

Her brain was in total chaos thinking about Pam's move

to Los Angeles being pushed farther away. Instead of being upset about having to pretend to be her sister even longer, she suddenly felt exhilarated knowing she had several more weeks with Jarrid!

She made a sharp turn into the parking structure for her last few hair appointments for the evening. She yanked open the door of the salon, verbally drilling into her skull the mantra, *Jarrid belongs to Pam. Jarrid belongs to Pam!*

Yet no matter how many times she said those words, she couldn't wait to be with Jarrid—for herself.

"Thank you so much for this order," Jarrid said, vigorously shaking Mr. Lyle's hand. "You'll be very pleased with the system my company will install."

Minutes later Jarrid was back in his van hurrying to make a few more customer calls. But he had only one thing in mind. He had to see Becky. He couldn't believe the rest of the words she had written in her special delivery letter. He needed to find out if she really meant what she had said.

In the early evening, after he finished work, Jarrid drove straight to the Beverly Hills salon. He parked his van at a metered spot and noticed that the shop was about to close for the night.

He looked through the glass door and saw Becky organizing her equipment at her station, ready to leave. With her letter tucked securely in his back pocket, Jarrid began to open the salon's door.

As Becky was about to head out, she came to a dead halt when she saw Jarrid opening the door to the salon. She panicked, not knowing what to do. She couldn't let anyone at work talk to Jarrid because someone might mention something about her past that had nothing to do with her twin's history.

She darted toward the front door, trying to get to him before he sauntered inside.

"Jarrid!" she said, leading him back outside to the sidewalk. "What an incredible surprise!"

"Becky, I got your letter," he said.

"My letter?" she asked, confused.

He pulled out a special delivery envelope from his back pocket. "You can't pretend with me this time," he said. "I've got the evidence right here."

Becky's thoughts suddenly went into a frenzy. A special delivery letter? She didn't send— Then she remembered her blinking answering machine. It had to be Pam. Her sister had said she was going to help her be more assertive with Jarrid. Had she sent a special delivery letter to Jarrid on her behalf?

Becky nervously fidgeted with her jingling car keys. "My letter, yes, of course. So what'd you think?"

"I don't know what to think, Becky," Jarrid said. "Your letter took me by surprise."

Her stomach was grinding. What did Pam put in that letter? "Did anything I say bother you?"

Jarrid held the envelope in his hand. "It's the way you said it."

The keys dug into her palm. "Exactly what way was that?"

Jarrid looked a bit surprised. "You want me to read it out loud?"

She swallowed and lifted her chin. "I'm not ashamed of what I wrote."

"Okay, if you really want me to."

Becky held her breath as Jarrid pulled out Pam's letter from the envelope, dreading to hear the contents.

Three

When Becky noticed Jarrid hesitate to read her sister's letter out loud, she felt even more insecure about what was inside.

"Becky, do you want me to skip to the lines that affected me the most?" he asked.

She was dying inside. "Those are my favorite parts."

He cleared his throat. "When I lie in bed at night, I fantasize about being in your arms." He glanced up at her. "Do you want me to go on?"

Her legs suddenly felt weak, and she leaned against the stucco building for balance.

"Sure, why wouldn't I?" She was going to strangle her sister.

Jarrid read on, "I think about your lips against mine. I think about your hands caressing my body all over. I need you, Jarrid. I need you so much." He slowly slipped the letter back into the envelope. "Do you really mean that, Becky?"

She tried to catch her breath. "Wh-why else would I have written it?"

She prayed he didn't hear the trembling in her voice. Because Pam's words were *exactly* how she felt about him.

Jarrid's eyes searched hers. "Are you sure you want to start something between us again?"

Start? She wanted to begin, continue and stay with him forever.

"Yes. I'm very sure, Jarrid." She could see the doubt in his eyes. Doubt she knew she had to wipe away for her sister. "I'll be right here for you, no matter how long it takes for you to trust me again."

Jarrid couldn't believe his ears. Becky was saying the words he longed to hear.

"What if I need months...years?" he asked, trying to contain the expectation rising in his heart.

"I'll wait decades, if that's what you need," she added, her eyes warm, inviting.

Jarrid wasn't thinking as he drew Becky to him. He needed to hold her, to feel her close to him. He pressed his face to her silken hair, breathing in the flowery scent of her. She smelled of full-bloomed roses, different from what he remembered. Sweeter, so much sweeter.

His mouth found hers. He felt her hesitate for a moment, but then her body relaxed against his. Her lips parted, and he blended his tongue with hers, exploring, tasting the honey of her.

As he drew her body even closer to his, he felt her full breasts crush against his chest. His tongue mingled with hers like a sensual dance of promises to come. He felt like he'd never kissed her before. He felt like she was a new woman to him.

"Hi, guys!" Sherry's voice rang out.

Jarrid was barely aware of standing on the sidewalk in front of the Nouveau Hair Salon. All he knew was that he didn't want to stop kissing Becky. He felt her lips slowly release from his, although his arms remained around her waist. Her cheeks were flushed. As he gazed into her eyes, she glanced away, almost like she was embarrassed by their kisses.

He held her close to him for a moment longer. "Have dinner with me tomorrow night," he dared to whisper.

A smile crossed her pink lips. "Yes," she whispered back.

Jarrid couldn't take his eyes off Becky as she introduced him to Sherry. She waved goodbye and followed her friend toward the parking structure.

He felt like the entire universe was in perfect alignment, remembering her words, *I'll be right here for you.* That is, until he remembered his commitment to meet Marie's friend on Saturday night at his brother's house.

A burning guilt filled his gut as he climbed into his van and slammed the door closed. A million excuses to tell Kenny and Marie why he couldn't be there flashed through his mind. But he couldn't hurt his sister-in-law. He'd made a promise to her, and he would keep it.

As he pulled out of the parking spot, he glanced behind to see if Becky was still in view. From a distance down the street, she turned and her eyes caught his. His heart swelled in his chest just looking at her.

Becky felt like she was walking on a fluffy cloud as she entered the parking structure with Sherry. Her cheeks grew hot thinking about Jarrid's intimate kiss. When his lips had first touched hers, she knew she should pull back. But she couldn't.

She'd wanted him to kiss her. She'd wanted to feel his hard body against hers. And when she'd felt his tongue meet hers, it was almost as if he were making love to her.

"Becky, you and Jarrid look perfect together," Sherry

said. "Why didn't you tell me that he was already very serious about you?"

When Becky heard the word *you*, a sinking feeling hit the pit of her stomach. Because she knew it wasn't her he felt close to. It was Pam.

"We're just friends," she quickly said as she got into her car.

"Friends?" Sherry repeated with a knowing smile as she opened her car door. "If my husband kissed me like that, we wouldn't leave our bedroom for twenty-four hours!"

Becky waved to Sherry and drove out of the parking lot feeling tense all over. She parked in her building's carport, feeling frustrated with herself. Why did she allow herself to believe that a man as incredible as Jarrid could ever be attracted to her?

She knew she wasn't exciting or sexy enough to hold the interest of any man. Even Darryl hadn't wanted to stay with her long enough to marry her.

Because two years ago, Becky discovered that she wasn't woman enough for any man.

As she sat in her car, she remembered the night Darryl severed their relationship. She had thought Darryl loved her. She had believed that someday he would ask her to marry him, although he hadn't introduced her to his family yet.

That fateful night, Darryl told her that he was working late at the health food store where he was a manager. She wanted to surprise him. But when she went to the store, she found another manager working the night shift.

Confused, she drove over to Darryl's apartment, but he didn't answer his doorbell. Feeling more upset by the minute, she hurried to the apartment of her best friend, Sarah.

Becky should have noticed Darryl's black car parked in front of Sarah's apartment building. She should have rung

Sarah's doorbell downstairs instead of going straight up to her apartment.

In Sarah's living room, Becky found Darryl with his shirt off. Sarah's hair was mussed, and she was only wearing a robe. Becky barely heard her best friend say she was sorry and that she didn't know how to tell Becky that she'd been secretly seeing Darryl for months.

All Becky heard was Darryl telling her that something vital was missing with her and that being with her had never been completely fulfilling to him.

"There's a sexual connection I feel with Sarah," Darryl sliced into her. "A passion I never had with you."

Becky felt betrayed. She felt devastated. But most of all, she felt like less of a woman. She didn't possess the sensual and emotional qualities to keep her man. And she knew why. She'd never felt excited or aroused when Darryl caressed her. She'd never even made love to him. But her best friend, Sarah, had.

Becky slammed her car door closed. The only man who had ever set her body temperature dangerously high was Jarrid Browning. But Jarrid didn't see her. He only saw her identical twin.

As Becky hurried to her apartment to call Pam and scold her about her special delivery letter to Jarrid, she spotted a large cardboard box at her doorstep with a receipt signed by her neighbor.

As she carried the box into her apartment, the telephone rang.

"Beck, I know you're mad at me about that letter," her sister said in a flurry, "but I was just trying to give the relationship a push."

"You mean a major shove!" Becky flopped onto the sofa. "Next time you plan to send Jarrid anything, you better discuss it with me first, okay?"

"I'm sorry I upset you, Beck," her twin said, concerned, but then added, "So? Is Jarrid warming up to you?"

Just thinking about Jarrid made her heart palpitate. "He asked me, I mean, you, out to dinner tomorrow night."

"Great, Beck!" Pam cooed. "I knew you'd win his heart for me."

Jarrid's sensual kiss plagued her. "Pam, I really need to tell you—"

"Did you read my diary?" her sister quickly cut in.

"Not yet." Becky quickly pulled Pam's thick mint green diary out of the box. "Is it X-rated?" she asked, trying to sound light, but inside, she felt uneasy about reading intimate details about her sister and Jarrid.

"Beck, don't worry, I never went all the way with him," her twin reassured her. "Jarrid is a sweetheart. Since I was just a high school student, he never went beyond making out."

Jarrid's respect for Pam made Becky feel even closer to him. "What else did you stick in this huge box?"

"You'll see," Pam said with a giggle.

Becky's eyes nearly popped out of her sockets as she fingered the nylon thong panties, see-through lace bras, skimpy sweater tops and low-necked dresses.

"Pam, I can't wear this stuff!" she shot out. "It's not me!"

"Exactly!" her sister insisted. "You won't be convincing if you go out with Jarrid wearing your cotton panties and loose tank dresses. He's a sexy guy. He enjoys being with a woman who's not afraid to reveal her sensual side."

I don't have a sensual side! she wanted to cry out, but was too ashamed to admit it, even to her identical twin.

"These dresses are too short, Pam," she protested. "I need to take down the hems."

"Don't you dare," Pam insisted. "I'll be in L.A. soon,

even with that delay Charlotte told me about. Can you hold out until then, Beck?"

Hold out? She wished she had an eternity to be with Jarrid. "I'll be fine," she told her.

When she hung up, Becky felt a grinding in her stomach. She wanted her sister to live in L.A. with her so badly. Yet, she wanted Jarrid, too.

She quickly opened Pam's diary and was glued to her fountain-penned words about Jarrid. Her sister wrote about how she fell for Jarrid at her girlfriend's sweet-sixteen party. About Jarrid's first tender kiss. About the yellow rose he put in her hair on their first Valentine's Day together.

Becky felt closer and closer to Jarrid as she got to know him through her sister's eyes.

She began reading something in the diary about Pam and Jarrid double dating, but part of the pages were smeared with spilled liquid, blotting out the words.

Then, her attention became riveted to the final pages. Pam wrote about her prom night when Jarrid gave her the miniature-diamond engagement ring in the back seat of the limousine he'd rented for their special night.

Becky bit her bottom lip as she read how Pam handed the velvet box back to him. How he was suddenly quiet. How he had stared out the side window for the rest of the ride.

Becky felt her own heart breaking in two, knowing how deeply hurt he must've been.

She set Pam's diary on her nightstand wishing she'd never read it. Because the more she learned about Jarrid, the deeper she fell in love with him.

Waiting at a Japanese restaurant in downtown Los Angeles, Jarrid glanced at his watch for the hundredth time. Becky was five minutes late. He knew he should've picked her up at her apartment. But she insisted on meeting him, saying something about her car being at the repair shop and Sherry giving her a ride. Now he wondered if she'd changed her mind about coming.

With his shoes off in traditional Japanese style, Jarrid sat at a low table on the tatami mat. He remembered that Japanese food was Becky's favorite and how she'd always dreamed of visiting Japan. He'd chosen a table in a private, secluded corner of the restaurant.

Just then, Jarrid spotted Becky enter the restaurant. He stood up at the sight of her. Her strawberry blond hair was piled high on top of her head. Her snug lavender dress hugged her shapely thighs as she removed her shoes and followed the polite Japanese host to the table.

Becky's shimmering oval eyes met his. "I'm sorry for being la—"

"Becky, you look stunning," he said, mesmerized by her beauty.

She blushed. "You do, too, I mean, what a great restaurant."

His fingers gently touched the warm skin of her arm. His gaze traveled down to her deep-cut lavender neckline revealing her fleshy cleavage. He felt the instant urge to press his lips against the valley of her breasts.

Take it real slow, real slow, he silently cautioned himself.

Jarrid took her hand and guided her to the low table on the floor. "Becky, should I order sushi for the two of us the way I always did?"

He waited as she quickly glanced at the menu and closed it. "Yes, of course, just like always."

"I'll ask the chef to prepare your tuna rolls the special way you like," he said, rising from the floor.

"Perfect," she replied.

As Becky watched Jarrid head toward the sushi bar, she suddenly felt in a major panic. She hated tuna! Her stomach felt queasy just thinking about eating it raw. But she had to if she was going to play her sister with him.

She shifted uncomfortably on her knees on the carpeted floor. Her sister's skintight lavender dress was strangling her breasts, hips and buttocks. The hem had ridden shamefully up to the very tops of her bare thighs. She'd nixed Pam's gray panty hose before she left her apartment because she liked her legs to feel free, but now she wished she'd worn nylons to cover up.

She shouldn't have listened to her sister about dressing sexy. She wished she'd worn her cotton bra, full-styled panties and loose tank dress, even if she did look reserved. It was better than dying of embarrassment wearing her twin's mini-dress.

When Becky knew no one was looking, she lifted up the lavender hem. She was relieved to see she had two inches of fabric to spare. She also noticed that the seams and hem of the dress were loosely sewn with thin single stitching. She quickly started pulling at the hem thread near both seams to lengthen the dress, even if the bottom of the dress would show a crease.

"Becky, the sushi looks—" Jarrid's gaze landed on her naked thighs. "Beautiful."

His sensual stare caused a pleasurable tingle between her legs. Her cheeks grew hot.

As she tugged the fabric over her bareness, she said, "I thought there was a stain on my dress."

"Can I help with anything?" he asked in a husky voice.

Could he ever! "Oh, no, everything's fine now."

As he sat down beside her on the floor, she was superaware of his broad shoulder leaning against her, and his muscled thigh pressing on her leg.

The waiter brought a delicately flowered plate containing rolls of raw tuna and white rice wrapped in dark green seaweed.

Becky nervously picked up her chopsticks. She wished Pam had written in her diary about tuna rolls being her favorite Japanese food. She would have had an alternate food request ready for Jarrid before he even mentioned the tuna.

Jarrid leaned closer to her and put a tuna roll on her plate. His face was near hers. She could smell the mint of his breath. She almost forgot the roll.

He waited for her to take the first bite. She reluctantly slipped it into her mouth.

"Ummmmm," she said, wanting to please him.

However, as she swallowed the raw fish, she felt the tuna instantly reverse back up her throat. About to gag, she quickly reached for her cup of water.

"Becky, are you okay?" Jarrid asked, concerned.

She started to nod yes for Pam's sake, but her head automatically shook no.

"Jarrid, I'm sorry," she burst out. "I don't like tuna."

"But I thought—"

She quickly added, "My taste in food has altered a little over the years. Doesn't everybody's?" She felt like she'd blown it for sure.

Jarrid gently brushed a speck of rice from her lips. "Becky, you've changed in a lot of ways. I like it." Then he grabbed her hand. "Come on, let's go get a hamburger."

She didn't know how she was going to arise from the floor in that constricting dress, so she bolted up. Suddenly, she heard a loud rip. The thin seams of her tight dress split apart on both sides from the hem up to her hips.

She felt a rush of air on her bare legs and buttocks. "Oh, no!" she cried out as she frantically grabbed the sides of her dress to hold it together, feeling so embarrassed she wanted to hide.

"Becky, take my jacket," Jarrid said.

He quickly removed his steel gray sports jacket and tied the sleeves around her waist. She felt completely taken care of as he graciously tipped the waiter and whisked her out of the restaurant.

In the windy, jasmine-scented Los Angeles evening, Jarrid protectively held Becky close to him as he handed the valet the ticket to get his van in the parking lot.

Becky began nervously biting her bottom lip. "Becky, don't worry," Jarrid whispered in her ear. "I'll get you home right away."

"Can anybody see anything?" she anxiously whispered back.

As Jarrid checked to make sure that his jacket sleeves were securely around her waist, a gust of wind blew his jacket up. He caught a glimpse of her firm, bare upper thighs, half-naked round buttocks and a wisp of pink thong panty.

Jarrid nervously pulled at his tight collar. His skin burned under his shirt. "You're very sexy, ahhh, covered."

Becky's surprised eyes looked up at him. "Do you really think so?"

"Think what?"

"About my being sex—" She stopped. "Being covered."

"Oh, yeah," he quickly replied, meaning yes to both.

She smiled. "Jarrid, thanks for taking care of me."

"Becky, I wish I could take care of you for—"

Before he could finish, a frizzy-haired woman and a tall man were suddenly at their side.

"Jarrid? Becky?" the woman asked, stunned. "I can't believe it's the two of you! Are you back together again?"

The New York accent and dimple on the woman's left

cheek made Jarrid immediately recognize her. "Connie Walker, what're you doing in L.A.?"

He thought he felt Becky stiffen beside him, and he figured she was uptight about her torn dress.

Memories of him and Becky double dating with Connie and his best buddy, Tim, in New York quickly rushed into his mind.

Connie smiled. "I'm Connie Jackson now and I'm living in Sherman Oaks with my husband, Joseph." She proudly held onto her man's arm. "Becky, it's so great to see you!"

Becky felt the blood drain from her face. "Connie, you look wonderful." Connie Walker. Connie Walker. She tried to remember seeing that name in Pam's diary but couldn't.

"Becky, do you recall the last double date you, me, Jarrid and Tim had together in New York?" Connie reminisced. "You never did tell me why you and Jarrid cut out early that night."

Becky panicked. "You're amazing, Connie, remembering that long ago."

The double date? She saw something about it in her sister's diary. Oh, no! The smeared pages! The pages containing the answers she needed to respond to Connie.

"Come on, Becky, tell me," Connie continued. "I'm dying to know what you two were up to."

Becky tried to think fast. "It probably wasn't very important because I can't even remember."

She felt Jarrid tense up beside her.

"That's right," he added. "A nothing-to-remember night."

His eyes caught hers. And she knew she'd said a horribly wrong thing.

Just then, the valet brought Jarrid's silver van. Becky breathed a sigh of relief.

"Connie, let's all of us get together again," he said.

"We're in the phone book under C. and J. Johnson," Connie said.

Becky hugged Connie, nodded to Connie's husband and climbed into Jarrid's van silently thanking the valet god for helping her escape another onslaught of Connie's probing questions.

However, as Becky sat in the bucket seat while Jarrid drove, she noticed how quiet he was. An uneasy feeling washed over her. She anxiously wrapped his jacket tighter around her body.

"Jarrid, my apartment is right off the Santa Monica Freeway," she said, trying to cut through the icicles. "Just six blocks from the Santa Monica Airport."

Jarrid glanced at her. "Becky, how could you forget what happened after we left the double date with Connie and Tim?"

His voice was low, disappointed. And for that moment, she hated herself for pretending to be her twin.

"I'm sorry, Jarrid," she quickly said. "I guess my mind was all boggled with my torn dress, and my brain went dead."

Jarrid stopped at a red light, rubbing his hands on the steering wheel, staring straight ahead.

"When we were finally alone that night," he began. "I parked my old Chevy alongside the Belt Parkway near the Verrazano Bridge."

Her hands were perspiring. "Yes, of course, near the Verrazano Bridge." She couldn't stand it! She needed her sister's help!

Jarrid hesitated. "It was the night I first told you that I loved you."

A car horn blared behind them, and Jarrid shot his van forward.

Becky stared out the side window seeing a blur. She'd hurt him, and she hadn't meant to. She wanted to tell him that she wasn't Pam. That she would never have forgotten the first time he said he loved her, not ever.

As Jarrid drove past the Santa Monica Airport, Becky stared at the private planes parked under the dark evening sky. She had to make things right again. For her sister, and for herself.

"Jarrid, can't we forget the past?" Becky asked. "It's over. I want to enjoy being with you now, right this very moment."

The strained lines on Jarrid's face slowly relaxed. He looked at her and smiled. "I'm up for that."

She could breathe again. "Great."

Jarrid parked his van in front of her apartment building and got out to open the door for her. "I can't wait to see your apartment."

Becky felt a panic attack coming on again as he followed her to her place. "Jarrid, it'll be much faster if I run in, get changed and run out."

What if he saw something un-Pam-like in her place? Besides, she hadn't been alone with a man in her apartment since Darryl, except for the electric guy because her electricity kept going out.

Jarrid stared at her. "Don't you trust me?"

"I, well—"

His sensual brown eyes held hers. "I promise not to watch you undress."

Her knees felt weak as she fumbled with her keys to unlock the door. "Come on in." Why did she feel like she *wanted* him to watch her undress?

She swung open the door. Her apartment was night dark. She flipped the light switch, but her living room remained in blackness.

"I just had the electrical lines checked," she said. "There's something wrong with the wiring, and sometimes the lights go on and off. I never know when."

Jarrid leaned over her to reach for the light switch, flicking it up and down several times. "Do you have a flashlight?"

His muscled chest rested against her back. With his hand on her waist, his other hand worked the switch. The heat from his body flowed through her muscles like a match lighting a candle. She instantly knew it was a mistake inviting him to her place.

"I've got a flashlight in the kitchen," she stammered.

"Let's go get it."

"I—I can't." She hesitated, feeling foolish. "I'm afraid of the dark." She was relieved knowing her twin was, too.

"That's right, I remember," Jarrid said. "I'll go find the flashlight, but first, let me try the switch again." He continued flicking the switch.

Her breathing quickened when she felt him move closer to her body. His fingers tightened around her waist. A hot sensation flashed through her when she thought she felt his manhood lightly press against her.

Just then, her apartment lit up. "There you go," he whispered, his warm breath against her hair.

Becky wanted to turn around and sink into his arms. Instead, while he wasn't looking, she grabbed the framed photo of her and Pam hanging on the wall and hurried toward the kitchen.

"Jarrid, can I get you a soda?" she called out.

"That'd be great," he said.

She hid the photograph inside a counter drawer and glanced back at Jarrid. He looked so comfortable in her place. She felt like he'd been at her apartment a million times before, and she couldn't imagine ever being without him.

As Jarrid stood in Becky's living room, he felt like he was catapulted into another dimension of her life. He remembered how lax Becky had been about neatness in high school.

Her school locker was always stuffed with crumpled sweatshirts, sweaters, books, munchy food crumbs, all in one big mess. Whenever she was in his old Chevy, she would absentmindedly leave torn tissues and scattered school paper on his car seat.

Jarrid was amazed at the transformation in her.

Becky's living room was immaculate. She had a cozy burgundy sofa with two white crocheted pillows on each end, a walnut coffee table with neatly piled magazines and a fluffy white rug in the center of the room.

"I never expected you to have an apartment like this," he couldn't help but say as she returned to the living room.

She put the soda cans down on the coffee table. "Don't you like it?"

He noticed her anxiously waiting for his response, as though his opinion meant more to her than anything else. He remembered that Becky always did what she did, no matter how anyone felt, including him.

"Does it matter what I think?" he asked, a bit surprised.

Her cheeks turned apple red. "I care very much, Jarrid."

His heart swelled. The sweetness of her caused him to take both of her hands and draw her into his arms.

"I love your place, Becky."

He kissed her forehead, the tip of her nose, and as he pressed his mouth to hers, her telephone rang.

For a moment Jarrid thought he saw a flash of alarm cross Becky's face.

"Excuse me," she quickly said. "I'll answer it in my bedroom while I get out of this dress."

"Sure," he replied as she hurried into her room and closed the door.

He felt a sudden uneasiness in his gut, as though she didn't want him to know who was on the phone. A burning sensation rushed through his bloodstream. Was Becky seeing another man?

Jarrid downed the carbonated soda in one gulp. He had no right questioning who was on her phone. She wasn't engaged to him. She could go out with whomever she pleased.

He blindly flipped through a magazine on her coffee table unable to stop thinking about the fact that he still couldn't trust how she felt about him.

He put down the magazine and took off his shoes. He was just about to lie back on her sofa with his hands behind his head when he stopped himself.

What am I doing? He realized he was acting like he was at home. Like she was his woman and he was her man.

He abruptly sat up. As he put his shoes back on, he was super-aware of her closed bedroom door blocking him out. He realized that he was letting her enter his heart too quickly, when he wasn't even sure where he stood with her.

He didn't dare hold her in his arms again. He didn't dare kiss or touch her. Because when her soft body was near his, he felt like she belonged with him forever.

Becky's eyes darted to her closed bedroom door. She anxiously pulled the phone closer to her lips. "Pam, I can't talk to you right now."

"Is Jarrid there?" her sister guessed in a rising voice of delight.

Becky's stomach fluttered with nervousness. "He's in the living room."

With her free hand, Becky untied Jarrid's jacket from around her waist, slipped off her torn dress and sat on her bed in her twin's lace bra and thong panties.

Pam excitedly said, "This is so great! Beck, what are you wearing?"

"I'm in your underwear," she replied and then stopped, realizing what her words insinuated to Pam. "I mean, the seams split apart on your dress, so I took it off and—"

"The seams split apart?" Pam giggled. "I like that one."

"Pam, I mean it!" Becky defended. "Nothing's going on between me and Jarrid." She still felt guilty about being in Jarrid's arms.

"Beck, I trust you," her sister said, tuning into her thoughts. "I want Jarrid to feel close to you because then he'll be close to me. I love you, sis."

"Pam, I love you, too." Becky desperately wanted to tell her twin that Jarrid was sinking into her skin. That she loved having him at her apartment.

"You better go back to Jarrid," Pam said. "I'll call you later." Then her sister's voice was gone.

Just as Becky hung up, her bedroom lights flicked off. The room was suddenly draped in jet-black. She heard a squeak like a mouse under her bed. From the corner of her eye, she thought she saw a creeping shadow enter her room through the window.

As she grabbed for the lamp switch in the dark, the lamp went crashing to the floor.

"Becky?" she heard Jarrid ask from behind the closed door.

Her heart raced in her chest. "I'm scared, Jarrid!"

Jarrid didn't wait for an invitation into her bedroom. In the next second, he opened her door. He could see her silhouette on the bed.

"Are you okay?" he asked worriedly.

She rushed into his arms. "Jarrid, hold me tight."

"Becky," he whispered, pressing his face against her hair, breathing the intoxicating bouquet of her. He felt her relax against him as though she trusted him completely.

Feeling very close to her, his lips drifted to her cheek, and then he found her mouth. He nibbled and licked and tasted her, wanting more, so much more.

He could feel her heartbeat thumping wildly as his tongue made love to hers. He pressed her body closer to him and felt the bare skin of her back. Her bra clasp was suddenly at his fingertips.

A jolt of desire fired through him. He realized that she was half-naked in his arms.

Jarrid forgot about his promise to himself. He forgot that he had to take it slow with her. All he could think about was how feverishly he needed her.

Four

Becky held her breath as she felt Jarrid unhook her bra clasp. She knew she should stop him. She knew she was going too far with him. But her body weakened with desire for his touch.

When she felt Jarrid's firm masculine hands cup her bare breasts, she heard a low moan escape from her lips. A pleasurable moan that was new to her. She wanted him to touch her in intimate places no man ever had.

She impulsively slipped her hands under his shirt, feeling the rippling muscles of his chest. She felt his heartbeat pound against her palms as though her touch had ignited his very being.

A groan rose from the depths of his throat as she fondled his nipples. His pleasure sounds caused a spark of flaming heat to flow throughout her body.

"Becky," he whispered, as he slid his palms down her bare back toward the silk of her panties. "I want to be close to you."

Her breath caught as he grasped her panty-covered buttocks in both hands pressing her against his growing manhood.

Suddenly the lights flashed back on in Becky's bedroom. She became acutely aware of her hands under his shirt, of his palms against her panty-covered derriere.

Her cheeks burned hot. She quickly slipped free of his arms and avoided his gaze. She reached for her torn dress on the bed to cover herself.

"Jarrid, it—it's getting late," she forced out. "I've got appointments early Saturday morning at the salon."

"Yeah, sure," he quickly said. "We'll get that hamburger another time."

Jarrid left Becky's apartment, carrying his jacket, feeling so much anxiety that he could barely unlock his van door. He hurled his jacket onto the front seat, frustrated and angry with himself.

He gunned up the engine. *You're going to shove Becky right out of your life again!* He'd planned on inviting her to his store again, but he hadn't gotten the chance. All because he'd allowed his yearning for her to get out of control.

He zipped off her Mar Vista street wondering if she would even want to see him again. That was the real problem. He never knew if he was doing the right or wrong thing with her.

Just moments ago, back in her bedroom, he was overwhelmed with desire for her. And he thought his need for her was as strong as her need for him. But maybe he was mistaken. Maybe he was so caught up in his longing for her that he was blind to the fact that she didn't feel exactly that way toward him.

As Jarrid headed toward his apartment, he realized that he was already seeing him and Becky as a couple again.

Stop assuming she wants you as much as you want her! he told himself over and over.

Jarrid knew one thing. He had to restrain his powerful feelings for her. Because if he didn't, his overpowering need to be close to her would scare her away forever.

In her bedroom Becky reached for the telephone to call Pam, but her hand froze on the receiver. She was still out of breath from Jarrid's steamy touch. Should she tell Pam that Jarrid had set her skin on fire? Could she share with her twin how sensual he made her feel and that all she could think about was making love to him?

Becky pulled her hand away from the receiver as though she might get electrocuted if she made the call. She couldn't phone Pam while her entire being felt like Jarrid Browning was the man she desperately wanted in her life. Her twin would immediately sense the truth, no matter how much she tried to hide it.

She went into the bathroom, and in the mirror she caught sight of her breasts exposed from Pam's unclasped lace bra. Her cheeks flamed with shame as she glanced down at Pam's scanty thong panties barely covering her femininity.

As she turned on the water faucet, a sadness waterfalled through her. She knew Jarrid would never have been in her bedroom if it weren't for his feelings for her sister.

She splashed cold water on her cheeks, trying to wash away her tender feelings for him, trying to figure out how she was going to make her sister understand that she never meant to end up in Jarrid's arms.

Saturday afternoon, as Jarrid lit the barbecue in Kenny's backyard, Becky filled his every thought. He had stopped himself several times from calling her since the evening of her apartment blackout.

He wanted to let her know that he wouldn't put any

pressure on her like he did seven years ago. He wanted to tell her that he would give her all the space she needed.

But he figured calling her to express those thoughts was a form of pressure in itself.

As he watched the barbecue flames penetrate the charcoal, he could see Becky's emerald eyes, her satin hair, smell her rose scent and feel the firmness of her buttocks in the palms of his hands.

"Are you looking forward to meeting Marie's friend?" his brother asked, setting the barbecue utensils next to the grill.

"Sure," Jarrid quickly replied, brushing away his intimate thoughts about Becky. However, in the process, he accidentally burned his finger on the hot barbecue. "Yow!"

Kenny swiftly handed him a cube from the ice chest. "Are you still pining over your old sweetheart?"

"I'm all mixed up, Kenny," he replied, applying the cold to his stinging finger. "Every time I think Becky cares the way I do, she puts on the brakes."

"You're trying too hard. Ease up a bit."

"How?" Jarrid felt the frozen ice sink into his finger, wishing he could cool down his hot emotions for Becky. "When I'm with her, she's got my heart in her hands. I can't help it."

"Uncle Jarrid, Mom's friend is here!" Lizzy dashed over to him, carrying a plateful of hamburger patties and hot dogs to grill.

Jarrid gulped. He felt like he was betraying Becky. The last thing he desired was to meet another woman, when deep down he only wanted Becky.

As he grabbed the plate from his niece, she nudged him down to her height and whispered in his ear, "My mom's friend is too starchy and stuffy for you, Uncle Jarrid."

Before he could respond, Marie walked over with her friend. "Jarrid, meet Leah Harris."

Jarrid extended his hand. "How are you, Leah?"

Her hand felt awkward in his, not warm and comfortable like Becky's did.

"A pleasure to meet you, Jarrid," Leah greeted him in a somewhat professional tone.

"Uncle Jarrid, I'm starving!" Lizzy announced, pulling him by the hand to the grill. "You make better burgers than my dad does."

Jarrid's brother pretended a long, hurt face, and Lizzy immediately went over to soothe his ego. Meanwhile, Jarrid put the meat on the hot grill.

He told himself to relax, but his thoughts were on Becky, wishing she was at the barbecue with him.

Leah sauntered over to him holding a glass of iced tea. She pointed to the only cheeseburger on the grill. "I would like mine medium rare."

"Sure." Jarrid searched for something to say to Leah. But his mind went blank. When he was with Becky, he was eager to share every single thought, every intimate feeling.

"Jarrid, did Marie mention that I have an ex-husband?" Leah said, cutting into his Becky thoughts.

"As a matter of fact she did," Jarrid replied as the charcoal smoke blew between them. He could barely concentrate on their conversation. The more Leah talked, the more he missed Becky.

"How long have you been divorced?" he asked, trying to keep a polite conversation going.

"Six months," she replied, her voice lowering. "We were married for eight years. I still think about him all the time. I miss him."

He knew exactly how she felt. "Really? I feel the same way about my old girlfriend."

"You do?" She looked relieved and quickly began talking about how her ex was the only man she ever truly cared about.

He flipped over her cheeseburger, realizing that Becky was the only woman he ever loved. The only woman he ever thought about. The only woman he could ever see himself with.

Just then, Jarrid noticed thick, black smoke gushing out of Leah's cheeseburger. "Geez!" he blurted, hurling the burnt-to-ashes burger into the trash can. "Leah, I'm sorry. How about a hot dog instead?"

Before waiting for her reply, he handed her a dog. Wanting to make up for his cheeseburger blunder, he tried to help by squeezing the mustard from its plastic container onto her frank roll.

Suddenly, the mustard burst out and splattered all over her perfectly spotless blouse. Her hands flew up. Her cup of iced tea sailed into the air, and the cold liquid splashed right into Jarrid's face.

Lizzy broke into uncontrollable laughter while Marie dashed into the house to get paper towels, and Kenny followed to answer the now-ringing telephone.

"Leah, I'll pay for the dry cleaning for your top," Jarrid said, wiping the icy-cold liquid dripping down his face. "I'm really sorry for the mess."

"So am I for your frosty-the-snowman face," Leah said as she frantically rubbed at the yellow stains on her blouse.

Just then, Jarrid heard Kenny calling, "Jarrid, you've got a phone call!"

He awkwardly excused himself and hurried inside. His technician, Pete, was on the phone. He'd asked Pete to work overtime on his day off so he could go to his brother's barbecue. Pete was always happy to put in extra hours at the store to get extra pay to support his family.

"Jarrid, I delivered the CD player and amplifier to Mr. Dunn's house like you wanted." Pete stopped talking as he went into a hacking cough. "But I had to go home before

I could install the equipment. I think I've got the flu. Could
you finish the job?''

"I'll leave right away."

"Mr. Dunn left his key in the usual spot," Pete added.
"Jarrid, I'm sorry for interrupting your day."

"Get to bed and feel better," he told him.

When he got off the phone and went into the backyard,
Leah had already left.

"Marie, I didn't mean to mess up your evening," Jarrid
began, feeling awful.

"You didn't," his sister-in-law said. "Leah said you
helped her to see that she's still attached to her ex-husband
and isn't ready to date anyone now. And from what Ken
told me the other night, you're still stuck on your old girlfriend, Becky."

"He told you that?" Jarrid abruptly shot his brother a
how-could-you-tell-her-when-I-told-you-not-to look.

Kenny sheepishly smiled, stuffed a hot dog into his
mouth and said no more.

Marie looked worriedly at Jarrid. "I don't want to see
you hurt by Becky again, Jarrid. I wish you would forget
her and start fresh."

"I don't know if I can, Marie." Jarrid knew she was
trying to protect him. But at that moment he had the sudden
urge to talk to Becky more than anything.

His niece walked arm in arm with him to the front door.

"Don't worry, Uncle Jarrid," Lizzy said. "I'll help you
find the perfect wife."

He gave her a squishy hug, loving her more than ever.
"I won't get married to anyone until I consult with you
first."

Before driving to his customer's house, Jarrid rushed
back to his apartment and immediately dialed Becky's
phone number. He had to know she was still in his life.

"Hello?" Becky's voice echoed in his ear.

Jarrid heard bubbling water in the background, not light sink water, but heavy bathtub water. He swallowed as he pictured her nude in the bathtub.

The words rushed out, the words that opened his heart wide to her. "I miss you, Becky."

The phone was silent for a long moment, and his heart sank. He shouldn't have called her. He was pushing himself on her again.

Lying naked in her vanilla-scented bathwater, after a long afternoon working at the salon, Becky held the portable phone to her ear. Her hands were trembling as she listened to Jarrid's deep voice needing her—needing Pam.

She pressed the phone closer to her lips. "Jarrid, I miss you, too," she dared to whisper back, not only for her sister, but for herself, too.

"Becky, I had to hear your voice."

She held her breath. "I'm so glad you called!"

"What are you doing right this very moment?"

"I'm taking a bath." Saying the word *bath* made her super-aware of her nudity, with Jarrid so close to her on the phone.

His voice lowered to a husky whisper. "Are you naked in the tub right now?"

"Completely," she responded, blood rushing to her face at her boldness. "I've got bubbles bursting all around my body.

"I wish I was in the bathtub with you," his manly voice whispered, grazing her ear like a physical caress.

A spasm of pleasure ran up her thighs, and she heard herself ask, "How would we fit? The tub's too small."

"I'd climb in the bath water first," he began, "and you could sit on my lap."

Her skin felt steamy from Jarrid's sexy words. Her taut nipples ached for his touch. The tender area between her legs pulsated with the need to be close to him. She gently touched her inner thigh dreaming of his hands on her skin.

The portable phone suddenly slipped from her wet fingertips and fell into the bubbly water.

"Oh, no!" She reached under the water and retrieved the phone. "Jarrid, are you still there?" She frantically shook the dripping receiver. "Jarrid?"

Hearing silence, she anxiously put the phone down on the floor and sank into the bubbly bath water wondering what to do. She didn't want him thinking she'd deliberately hung up on him because of his sensual talk. Yet she didn't dare call him back on another phone because then he might think she was encouraging him, which is exactly what she wanted to do!

Her body was still pulsating with desire from his sexy words. She wasn't sure how long she lay in the tub thinking about Jarrid when she heard the doorbell ring. She climbed out and wrapped a terry towel around her wet body.

She ran to the front door and looked through the door viewer. Her blood rushed like hot lava through her veins when she saw Jarrid standing outside her door.

His curly hair was a little mussed. His brown eyes looked worried. He nervously stuck his hands in his pockets, as though he wasn't sure she would open the door for him.

Without a second thought, Becky yanked open the door, forgetting her half-naked state, forgetting she was supposed to be her sister.

"Jarrid, I didn't mean to hang up on you," she said.

His eyes held steady on hers. "I thought you were mad at me about the bathtub conversation."

"Oh, no, never." The words came out before she could stop them. "I wanted to hear more."

Her face flamed at her admission. She noticed his gaze slowly travel down her towel-covered body.

Becky secretly wanted Jarrid to tear off her towel and

caress her aching skin. But from the corner of her eye, she saw the framed picture of her and Pam that she'd put back on her living room wall.

She quickly positioned the front door to block Jarrid's view of the photograph. Feeling hot guilt over her sensual thoughts about him, she drew the towel tighter around her throbbing body.

"Becky, I didn't come here to make you uncomfortable," Jarrid gently said. "My technician's out sick, and I need to install some equipment at a customer's house. Want to go with me?"

"Now?" she asked, unable to hide her excitement that he'd come over because he wanted to be with her. "Won't your customer mind if I tag along?"

"Not at all, I've worked for him before," he quickly replied. "He's out of town and wants me to install the equipment while he's away." He gently pushed back a wet strand of hair from her eyes. "Will you come?"

Would she ever! "Sure, I'd love to. But I've got one problem."

He frowned. "What's that?"

"I can't go in this towel."

A slow grin crossed Jarrid's face, as though he wouldn't mind at all. "How about if I wait in my van for you?"

"I'll be out in a sec!"

The moment Jarrid was gone, she hurriedly threw off the towel. She searched her closet for something to wear, wanting to look pretty for Jarrid. Then she saw Pam's mint green, flowered, spaghetti-strap summer dress draped on a hanger with a note pinned on the back saying, "Wear for Jarrid, without a bra."

After her Japanese restaurant experience, Becky hesitated on the spaghetti straps. Yet, she needed a stark reminder that she was with Jarrid for her sister, so she wouldn't get caught up in her own feelings for him.

Becky slipped on the dress without a bra and draped a shawl around her shoulders. *I'm going to be Pam, Pam, Pam!* she told herself over and over.

Yet she was so nervous and excited about spending time with Jarrid that she almost forgot her apartment keys!

Outside Becky's apartment building, sitting in his van, Jarrid anxiously tapped his fingers on the steering wheel. Seeing Becky wrapped in that towel and imagining her totally naked underneath had pumped his blood so strong that he had to hold himself back from slipping the towel off her.

Jarrid didn't remember ever wanting Becky as much seven years ago as he wanted her now.

Ease slowly back into her life, he reminded himself. *If I show her how badly I want to be with her like I did in the past, I'll frighten her off.*

Just then Becky hopped into his van wearing a low-necked dress that revealed a hint of cleavage with a light shawl wrapped around her shoulders.

"Hope I wasn't too long," she said, her sweet feminine voice singing in his ear.

The scent of roses filled his van. He noticed the outline of her thighs under the soft fabric of her dress. He swallowed and kept his hands firmly on the steering wheel so he wouldn't reach out and caress her.

Inside the customer's hilltop house in Sherman Oaks, Becky enthusiastically helped Jarrid carry cables and wires to the second floor of the all-glass modernistic structure.

As Jarrid lifted the carousel CD player onto the shelf, Becky assisted him. She tried not to notice his bare arm muscles flexing as he worked. She tried to ignore the heat of his body so close to hers and her desire to be snugly encased against him.

Jarrid momentarily glanced at her. "Becky, you're so quiet."

"I was just thinking about you, I mean, about your home entertainment business."

He tilted his head with a twinkle in his sexy brown eyes. "Really? How come your cheeks are all red?"

She touched the heat of her face. "I guess it's getting a little warm in here."

Jarrid put down the wires and took her hand. "I'll cool you down," he said, leading her out to the balcony.

The early evening desert breeze gently blew back her hair as she gazed at the shimmering lights of Los Angeles.

"How beautiful," she whispered.

He was staring at her. "Yes, very beautiful."

She felt his hand slip around her waist and draw her close to him. She tried to concentrate on the glittery balcony view, but her skin temperature soared from being near him.

"You've got a great business, Jarrid," she said, trying to swerve her thoughts away from the shivers of his touch. "I bet you have tons of customers wanting you to design their home entertainment systems."

"That's my dream, Becky," Jarrid said. "I want to open a mega store someday. But I've been having trouble connecting with people who can afford my custom designs."

His hand gently moved up and down her back, making it almost impossible for her to think about anything but her longing to be more intimate with him.

"Maybe I can help," she offered, wanting to do anything she could to get closer to him.

"How?"

"My clients at the salon are either successful businesswomen or married to wealthy men," she said. "I'll tell them that you design home theater systems. I bet I can get you new customers."

Jarrid looked at her, a bit surprised. "You'd do that for me, Becky?"

"Of course!" *I'll do anything to make you happy,* she wanted to add. "Give me your business cards and store pamphlets and—"

Jarrid cupped her face between his hands. "You're amazing, you know that?"

She impulsively circled her arms around his neck. "So are you!" She meant it because Jarrid made her feel indispensable to his life.

She suddenly realized that her lips were close to his. She felt his palms against her back, pressing her closer to him. In the next moment his mouth found hers.

Jarrid's heart overflowed with love for Becky as he kissed her. He couldn't believe how responsive she was to sharing his dream.

When he gazed into her eyes, she looked up at him with a caring that made him desire her even more. He slipped the shawl from her shoulders and kissed her throat. He glided his lips to the swell of her breasts over the top of her dress. He tasted and nibbled the sugary flesh of her, needing and wanting more of her.

He slipped his fingers under the thin straps of her dress and slid them down her shoulders. He felt her breathing quicken as he lowered the fabric until her bare breasts were exposed. He cupped her firm breasts in the palms of his hands.

"Becky, you feel so good to me, so good," he groaned, covering one hard nipple with his mouth. He pressed his face between her full mounds, kissing the deliciousness of her.

He felt her tremble as he tenderly slid his hand under the hem of her dress and glided his fingers to the inside of her soft thighs. His manhood responded as he neared the patch of panty covering her femininity.

Her breath caught as he gently touched her feminine spot over the cotton, feeling closer to her than he ever had before.

He heard a moan escape from her lips, and then she breathlessly whispered, "Jarrid, I—I'm not sure."

With his heart hammering against his ribs, he gently released her. She quickly slipped the top of her dress back on.

More than anything, he didn't want her to emotionally pull away from him.

"Becky, do you want me to take you home?" he asked.

"I think so," she responded, a bit unsurely.

As he began packing up his tools, she was right there helping him. He wanted to tell her that every kiss, every touch he shared with her made him feel more deeply connected to her.

Yet, how could he express those feelings without revealing his intense desire to share a future with her. He still wasn't sure about her feelings for him.

Five

As Jarrid drove her home, Becky felt overwhelmed by how intimately close she felt to him. His hands on her body had made her feel like his woman, his love. And it scared her.

Burning at her brain was one question. Had she kissed Jarrid to help her sister's relationship with him? Or had she melted without resistance into his arms solely because of her own sensual and emotional desire to grow closer to him?

Her fingers trembled as she took out her key in front of her apartment. Jarrid was standing so near her that all she could think about was inviting him inside. But she didn't dare.

He lifted her chin and looked into her eyes. "Becky, I want you to know something," he began. "That blind date my sister-in-law arranged for me—"

"You don't have to tell me, Jarrid."

She knew she had no right to feel jealous about the man

her twin was in love with. Yet her insides crunched thinking about him being with his sister-in-law's friend.

"I want you to know what happened," he went on. "The entire time I was talking to her, all I thought about was you."

"You did?" she asked, unable to believe it, remembering how Darryl had turned his affections to her best friend because she wasn't enough for him.

"I kept wishing you were with me," he added.

Without thinking, Becky kissed him on the lips. "Jarrid, you make me feel so special!"

Before he could respond, she hurried into her apartment and leaned against the closed door, feeling an ecstatic happiness she'd never known before. Jarrid had thought about *her* on his date tonight. He made her feel like the highlight of his life. He was perfect for her, so perfect.

At the salon during the week, Becky couldn't think of anything but Jarrid. She excitedly handed out his business cards to all of her clients. She praised his work and said he was the most sought-after home theater designer in Los Angeles.

She suggested that if her clients wanted a custom-designed system they should hurry and call Jarrid at the store before he got too booked up.

Then one morning her wealthy client, Mrs. Morton, told Becky that her husband might be interested in Jarrid's work and wanted to call him. She could barely contain her delight as she gave Mrs. Morton his business card.

Late Friday afternoon Becky excitedly finished styling her last client's hair. She was going to surprise Jarrid at his store. She had to find out if Mrs. Morton's husband had called him. Besides, she couldn't wait to see him again!

Jarrid was elated as he hung up the telephone at his store. He turned to Pete who was setting a newly arrived VCR on the shelf for display.

"You won't believe this," Jarrid began. "Jack L. Morton just called. He wants to meet me."

"*The* Mr. Morton, owner of the chain of Pure Health Food stores throughout California?" Pete asked as he coughed and blew his nose.

"That's the man," he replied. "He invited me to a party tonight at his house in Redondo Beach. He wants to discuss my designing a movie mini-theater for his home."

"All right!" Pete said enthusiastically. "How'd you connect with a bigwig like J. L.?"

"Through Becky," Jarrid said, still unable to believe it, telling Pete about how she had been recommending him to her clients.

Pete grinned. "Looks like your relationship with Becky is finally working out the way you want."

"I sure hope so, Pete." He was afraid to be overly confident where Becky was concerned. He knew how easily her feelings could change. "Pete, why don't you go home, drink some hot tea and get to bed early. I can handle the store myself until closing time."

"Good luck with Mr. Morton," Pete said. "*And* with Becky!" Then he left.

As Jarrid greeted a couple of customers who entered the store, he inwardly smiled. Becky had kept her promise. He was sure that her enthusiasm about his business was a super sign that she wanted to become a major part of his life.

As Becky parked her car in front of Jarrid's store, she gazed up at the neon sign above the door flashing, *Browning's Home Entertainment Systems.*

She felt so proud of him!

She quickly got out and opened the glass front door of his store. Inside, she saw a couple of customers wearing earphones testing out the sound systems. The walls were lined with shelves displaying black and silver high-tech audio/video receivers, laser disc players, carousel CD players and different-shaped speakers.

She spotted Jarrid in the back showing a male customer a sleek amplifier. He didn't see her as he intently demonstrated the component.

Becky wanted to put her arms around Jarrid's waist, lean her head against his shoulder and listen to his great sales technique.

She noticed a customer waiting at the cash register to purchase some cables. Seeing how busy Jarrid was, she quickly set down her bag and hurried over to the register to help the man. She knew how to use the register because she sometimes had to fill in at the salon when the receptionist was out.

She glanced at Jarrid, hoping he wouldn't mind her jumping in and helping out.

Just then Jarrid momentarily caught her gaze. His eyes lit up, and a broad smile crossed his face, like it was natural for her to be in the store with him, like she'd been in his life forever.

With a jolt of energy, she rang up the customer's item.

Jarrid pointed to the five-channel power amplifier. "This stereo amplifier combines low distortion and flat frequency response," he explained to his customer, glancing over at Becky as she busily worked at the cash register and chatted pleasantly with a customer.

His heart swelled. For a split second, she felt like his wife. Mrs. Becky Browning. He liked the sound of her first name linked with his last name. If she wanted to keep her own last name, that would be okay with him, too.

A surge of electricity powered through his body as he

continued talking to his customer. Her coming to his store meant more than she could ever know.

Before Becky realized it, customers left for closing time. She saw Jarrid lock up the front door, and then she felt his hands slip around her waist and gently draw her against him.

"Becky, I could get used to having you at the store with me all the time," he whispered as his lips tenderly touched hers.

"So could I," she confessed, weakening with love for him.

"When can you start?" he teased, lightly biting her bottom lip.

"Whenever you want me to," she teased back, kissing him, wanting to remain in the cocoon of his strong arms for as long as she could.

When he released his mouth from hers and tenderly ran his fingers through her hair, he said, "The customer you referred to me called today."

"Mr. Morton?" she asked excitedly. "What did he say?"

"He wants to hear my ideas on a custom-designed theater system for his house!"

"Oh, Jarrid, that's great!" She hugged him tight. "Don't worry. I'll get you more customers. I'll make sure you're bombarded with calls. You'll be the most successful—"

His mouth covered hers before she could finish. She felt united with him in a way she never dreamed she could with a man.

In between kisses, he said, "Mr. Morton invited me to a party at his house tonight to celebrate the grand opening of his natural foods store in Sherman Oaks." His eyes glowed with love for her. "Will you go with me?"

"Jarrid, I wouldn't miss it!" she exclaimed, hugging him tighter.

A little while later, Becky was rushing into her apartment to get ready for the party. She beamed with happiness that Jarrid might get a job designing a home entertainment system for Mr. Morton because of her.

As she searched her closet for something dazzling, beautiful and sensual to wear for Jarrid, she began plotting to send him more customers so his dream to open a larger store would come true.

She inwardly smiled, almost feeling like his business agent. She loved helping him. She loved being with him. She loved—

Just then, the telephone rang.

"Beck, I'm on my way to L.A.!" her sister's voice echoed in her ear over the phone.

"When?" She suddenly felt like there was no air in her bedroom.

"Charlotte called," her twin hurried on. "My new job is available whenever I'm ready. I've got one more big account to finish here in New York, and then I'll be leaving to be with my favorite sister!"

Jarrid flashed in her mind. Jarrid, the man she wanted. The man that belonged to her sister.

"Pam, I can't believe you're finally coming!" she said, feeling a rush of anxiety and exhilaration all at once.

"There are so many things I want to share with you when I move to L.A.!" her sister went on.

"Me, too!" She wanted to spend hours and hours with her twin, making up for all those years they were kept apart.

"I better get some shut-eye," Pam said. "Tomorrow, I'll be interviewing candidates for my New York job. Talk to you later!"

Becky didn't remember hanging up. Conflicting thoughts ricocheted through her head. She couldn't wait to be with her sister, yet at the same time she wished she wasn't coming. What was she going to do about her overwhelming love for Jarrid?

In a turmoil, she went into the living room, not knowing what to do. She lifted the photograph of her and Pam off the wall to look at it. Now she and her identical twin would finally be a real family.

When she went to hang it back on the wall she missed the hook, and the picture went crashing to the floor. She watched in horror as the wooden frame broke apart and the glass cracked. She picked up the precious photograph, relieved that it was unharmed. She held the photograph tight against her chest feeling crushed from both sides and seeing no escape.

Jarrid's adrenaline was pumping through his veins as he parked his silver van in front of Becky's apartment building.

He turned off the engine, trying to calm his heated expectations. He couldn't help feeling that maybe, just maybe, he was going to end up marrying Becky.

He got out of the van wearing a crisp button-down white shirt, a suit jacket and finely pressed pants. Before he closed the van door, he reached for the yellow rose he bought for her hair, remembering the yellow rose he'd given her on their first Valentine's Day together.

Holding the rose behind his back, Jarrid knocked on Becky's apartment door. When she opened it, he sucked in his breath at the glittering beauty of her.

Her hair was flowing down her shoulders. A form-fitting gold dress hugged her small waist and shapely hips.

He swallowed, wanting to close the door behind them, draw her into his arms and make love to her.

"Becky, you look gorgeous."

Her cheeks turned crimson. "I do?"

"Oh, geez, yeah."

He was so caught up in her beauty that he almost forgot the flower.

"I brought you a yellow rose," he said, revealing it from behind his back.

For a moment he thought he saw a flash of sadness in her eyes, but then she smiled.

"Jarrid, it's beautiful," she said, leaning forward to smell the delicate flower.

As she bent over, her ivory breasts gushed above the strapless golden dress. He could feel his fingers perspiring against the stem of the flower.

"Can I put the rose in your hair?" he asked.

She nodded as her alluring eyes gazed up at him. He gently parted the silk of her perfumed hair. Her glittering body was only inches from his touch. His blood rushed through his body at high speed as he slipped the flower into her satiny strands.

"Becky, I hope we're never apart again," he whispered, unable to hold back his feelings for her.

When she was silent for a long moment, he felt a bit uneasy.

"Becky, is anything wrong?"

"Oh, no," she quickly said. "Everything's perfect."

Yet as Jarrid led Becky to his van, doubts loomed up in his brain. Was she thinking about eventually leaving him or were his past insecurities with her making him doubt the solidity of their relationship?

At the crowded party, Becky gently touched the rose in her hair, remembering its significance from Pam's diary.

Her heart ached knowing she had so little time left with him.

As soft music filled the spacious living room of the party, she felt Jarrid squeeze her hand. His eyes held hers as though he was silently telling her that he saw them as a couple, solid and connected inside.

She squeezed back his hand because she felt that way, too.

Guests said hello to her and Jarrid. Managers from Mr. Morton's various natural food stores shook their hands. Someone mentioned that the new manager of the store opening in Sherman Oaks would be arriving soon.

However, Becky couldn't concentrate on anyone but Jarrid. She wanted to desperately hold on to the precious moments she had remaining with the man she loved.

"Becky!" she heard Mrs. Morton call out, walking over with a distinguished elderly gentleman at her side. "I want you to meet my husband."

"Hello, Mr. Morton," she graciously said, feeling a little nervous, wanting Jarrid to get the job. "This is Jarrid Browning."

As Jarrid and J. L. Morton made their acquaintance, his wife excused herself to greet some guests who'd just arrived. Becky kept her fingers crossed behind her back, hoping that Jarrid and Mr. Morton would click.

Suddenly Becky's body went numb. Across the room, standing with Mrs. Morton, was her ex-boyfriend, Darryl. He had an attractive redheaded woman close by his side.

"Becky, I hope you don't mind if I borrow Jarrid for a few minutes," Mr. Morton said, interrupting her chaotic thoughts.

"Oh, not at all, Mr. Morton," she quickly replied.

Jarrid kissed her softly on the lips. "With you here, I've got all the luck I need." Then he walked to the other side of the room with Mr. Morton.

Becky felt like she couldn't breathe. *What's Darryl doing here?* Then she remembered that when she dated him, Darryl had worked as a manager of a health food store named Pure Health Foods, which was one of Mr. Morton's.

She saw Darryl walk over to Mr. Morton to shake his hand. She felt the room spinning as their host introduced him to Jarrid.

As she stood frozen to the floor, she noticed Darryl momentarily turn away from his companion and start eye flirting with another woman in the room.

A sickening feeling hit her gut. Darryl, who had deserted her for her best friend, now had a new woman and was openly tease gazing with another female.

She realized that he couldn't be loyal to any woman. In that instant, she understood that maybe it wasn't all her fault that their relationship had fallen apart.

She glanced over and saw Mr. Morton being drawn into a conversation with another guest. Her insides crunched when Jarrid and Darryl started talking to each other.

Becky's eyes darted in every direction, looking for the powder room, needing to get out of view until Darryl was away from Jarrid.

"Becky!" she heard Jarrid call out, waving her over to him.

She wanted to shake her head no. She couldn't go to him. But she didn't want him to get suspicious. So she forced herself to walk toward him, feeling lightheaded and faint, praying her dream world with Jarrid wasn't about to crumble into tiny pieces.

As Becky neared him, Jarrid thought he saw a streak of panic in her eyes.

"Becky," he said, slipping his fingers through hers. "Meet the manager of the new Sherman Oaks store. This is—"

"How are you doing, Becky?" Darryl cut in.

Jarrid's stomach tightened in a knot as he heard the intimate familiarity in Darryl's tone.

"I'm just great, Darryl," Becky replied in a shaky, strained voice.

"You two know each other?" Jarrid asked, trying to keep his voice light. He felt hot with emotion thinking that another man had gotten as close to Becky as he had.

"Becky and I were a steady item for a while," Darryl replied. "Weren't we, Becky?"

"For a very short time, Darryl," she replied, her eyes nervously darting toward Jarrid.

He could barely hear the music or the guests' laughter at the party. All he was aware of was how uncomfortable she looked, and he wished he knew why.

Darryl turned to his girlfriend. "I'm sorry, Marilyn. This is Becky Pierson."

Pierson? Jarrid silently repeated, confused. He knew that her last name Lawson was her birth mother's surname. However, Pierson was not the adopted name she had when he knew her in high school.

His speculations were cut off by Mr. Morton, who was calling for the attention of his guests.

"I would like to make a toast," J. L. Morton announced, holding up a glass of champagne. "To the opening of my Sherman Oaks store in Los Angeles and to the new manager, Darryl Burton!"

As Darryl and his lady friend walked over to Mr. Morton, Jarrid anxiously looked at Becky, feeling confused and needing to understand what was going on.

"Why did Darryl call you Becky *Pierson?*" he forced out.

Becky's throat constricted, and for a second she couldn't talk.

"He must be mixed up," she stammered, struggling for a logical explanation.

"What do you mean?" Jarrid asked.

"He learned about my new birth name right before we

broke up," she replied. "I guess he's had so many girl-friends since then that he couldn't correctly remember my new last name."

"Becky, why didn't you tell me about him before?"

"Because Darryl hurt me," she blurted.

She hadn't wanted to say that. The only person she'd ever told about Darryl's rejection of her was her twin. Even then, she'd been too ashamed to go into detail about his blistering remarks about her inadequacies as a woman.

"What did he do to you?" Jarrid's voice shook a little, as though her past hurt had suddenly become his own.

"I found out that he was making love to my best friend behind my back." Her eyes clouded at the memory. "I thought he cared about me, but—"

Before she knew it, Jarrid's arms were around her.

"Becky, Becky," he whispered in her ear. "I can't imagine wanting any woman but you."

His words were like a soothing ointment, because she knew he would never be unfaithful to her.

Just then she saw their host trying to catch Jarrid's attention.

"You better go," she said. "Mr. Morton is signaling you."

"I can't leave you now," he said.

"Go," she urged him, kissing him gently on the lips. "Get that job."

As he reluctantly walked through the party crowd toward Mr. Morton, she knew Jarrid would never hurt her. He was the most loyal man she'd ever met. She almost wished she had never met him. Now she knew how wonderful it felt being with a totally devoted man, and in a little while, she'd have to live without him.

As Jarrid sifted through the crowd, he could still feel Becky's pain from Darryl's infidelity. He wanted to bag the guy right then and there.

His eyes landed on Darryl. He was holding a red Bloody Mary drink in his hand, piously standing beside his girl-friend, conversing with the guests.

Unable to hold back his anger, Jarrid slipped through the packed party people and "accidentally" knocked into his arm, sending the glass of blood red liquid splashing down the jacket of his immaculate beige designer suit.

"Excuse me," Jarrid said, feeling an inward satisfaction at the horror on Darryl's face as he wiped at the mess.

Jarrid walked over to Mr. Morton on the other side of the room and began explaining how he would set up his living room with front left-right and surround bi-directional speakers, a drop television screen, power amplifier and dig-ital satellite dish.

However, his thoughts kept shifting to Becky. He couldn't help but wonder if her hesitation to get involved with him had something to do with the anguish that Darryl had caused in her life.

"Jarrid, when can you start the work?" Mr. Morton asked.

"Is tomorrow too soon for you?" he asked.

"Sounds like a solid plan to me," J. L. replied, firmly shaking his hand.

Jarrid practically flew through the party guests to tell Becky.

Her eyes widened with expectation. "Well?" she asked.

"Mr. Morton hired me for the job!"

"Oh, Jarrid, I knew he would!" She jumped into his arms and covered his lips with hers.

As Jarrid returned her kiss, he knew he was ready to take the next step with her. He wanted to introduce her to his family.

However, he had one big problem. How was he going to get Kenny and Marie to want to meet her?

He knew the memory of Becky's rejection was plastered in their minds, especially with Marie. He knew that she didn't want him seeing Becky at all.

Yet, he had to take the chance and ask them, anyway.

A few days later he went to his brother's house to install new surround sound speakers in their living room. He was standing on a ladder. Marie was watching him from below. His brother reached into the tool box for a screwdriver he needed.

His body felt tense. He could hardly concentrate on hooking up the wires. He was glad that Lizzy was at a friend's house, so he could talk to Marie and Kenny alone.

"Jarrid, it's so nice of you to put in these new speakers for us," Marie said excitedly.

Jarrid could feel Kenny's suspicious eyes on him. His brother *always* knew when something was up.

"Nice of him?" his brother began, handing him the screwdriver. "I asked him three months ago to put in new speakers for us."

"Come on, Ken," Marie protested. "Your brother's doing us a favor."

"I say he's here because he wants something."

"Well, actually," Jarrid said, clearing his throat as he came down the ladder. "I did want to ask you two a question."

"You see? I knew it!" his brother exclaimed. "These speakers come with a price."

"Jarrid, don't listen to him," his sister-in-law said. "*I* appreciate your taking the time to do this for us. So ask whatever you please."

"I want you to meet Becky."

"Becky?" Marie repeated, glancing with concern at

Kenny. "I thought you were going to forget her and go on with your life."

"I can't, Marie." He looked at his brother for support. "She's on my mind all the time."

Kenny put his arm around his wife. "Marie, I think he's got it bad for her."

Marie wasn't listening. "Jarrid, she broke your heart in two. You're putting yourself in the same vulnerable position again."

"Becky's different now," Jarrid rushed on. "She's almost like a new woman to me."

"Has she talked about wanting to marry you?" Marie asked. "Has she discussed having your children someday?"

All of Jarrid's doubts suddenly surfaced. "No, not yet, but—"

"You see?" Marie turned to her husband. "She's going to hurt him again, Ken. I can feel it."

His brother put on a jazz CD to try out the new speakers. "Marie, how do we know what her intentions are unless we meet her?"

"Kenny's got a point," Jarrid quickly agreed. "If you meet Becky face-to-face, you'll see what a terrific woman she is."

"What if I don't like her?" she asked. "What if I sense that she's not serious and might break up with you again? I won't sit quietly."

"I'll take that chance," Jarrid said, hoping he was doing the right thing.

"Okay, all right." She surrendered. "Invite her to dinner next Sunday."

"Kenny, you married a fine lady!" he said.

"Don't I know it," his brother said, winking affectionately at his wife.

Jarrid watched Marie snuggle into his brother's arms.

From the cuddly way she rested her face on his chest, he knew she'd never leave Kenny, because she was an integral part of him.

As he jumped into his van to go home, he wondered if Becky would ever feel that way about him. Back at his apartment, his plans to call her were interrupted by his blinking answering machine.

"Hi, Jarrid!" Becky resonated on the tape. His pulse immediately went into high gear just hearing her voice. "I think I may have another customer for you," she went on. "My hair client, Mrs. Harrison, said her husband, who's the CEO of Jenkins Telecommunications, wants a huge entertainment system installed in their Santa Barbara weekend house." Her voice rose with excitement. "Jarrid, this job could be a biggie! I'll let you know when I hear more."

Jarrid felt a jolt of energy. Why doubt it? He felt that she was sending him a clear message that she wanted to be a steady part of his daily existence.

He was about to pick up the phone to call her back but then stopped. *I should let Becky enter my life at her pace, not mine,* he told himself.

He would tell her about Marie and Kenny's dinner invitation tomorrow. Maybe meeting his family would make her view the two of them as a family, too.

At the Nouveau Hair Salon, Becky could barely contain her glee. She finished her hair-cutting appointment, and the next scheduled one was in two hours.

She quickly glanced through the front window of the salon and saw Mrs. Harrison and her husband waiting in his shiny black Mercedes to follow her to Jarrid's store.

She had tried calling Jarrid that morning, but Pete told her he was at Mr. Morton's Redondo Beach house designing his home theater system and would be back at noon.

She left a message that the Harrisons would be at his store at four o'clock.

As Becky grabbed her bag, she heard Sherry's voice behind her. "From the enthusiastic way you're promoting Jarrid's business," she began, "anyone would get the distinct impression that you're very much in love with him."

I am! she wanted to exclaim, but instead, she said, "Since I've got the right connections, I want to help make Jarrid's home entertainment business the best in L.A."

"You're definitely giving him the right signal," her friend commented.

"What signal is that?"

"You want to marry him," she replied, glancing at her watch. "Gotta go. I'm making dinner for my in-laws tonight."

As her friend left, Becky realized that she *was* acting like she wanted to be his wife. She couldn't hide it. That's exactly the way she felt about him!

Jarrid glanced out the front window of his store waiting for Becky to arrive. He had decided to close the store a little earlier so he could give his full attention to Mr. Harrison. He sent Pete to J. L. Morton's house with another technician he just hired, to install the components for the system he'd designed that morning.

He straightened the speakers on the shelves. He was nervous about inviting Becky to his brother's house. Her answer would tell him if she wanted to go in the same direction with their relationship as he did.

Just then he spotted Becky's VW Rabbit drive up to the curb with a Mercedes right behind. A few minutes later the door of his store opened, and Becky walked inside.

His soul instantly lit up in her presence. She made quick introductions, all the while glancing at him with a warmth in her eyes that made him wish he was alone with her.

Jarrid answered Mr. Harrison's extensive questions and listened to his audio and video needs. Then he showed Mr. Harrison samples of sketches he'd done.

"I can install surround sound speakers and video monitors in every room of your Santa Barbara house," Jarrid explained. "I'll put in infrared leads so you can walk from room to room with one remote and control the picture, sound and music from wherever you are in your house."

"Very, very impressive," Mr. Harrison commented, showing the sketches to his wife. "However, I would like you to see the setup of my weekend home so you can give me specifics geared to the unique style of my house."

"Absolutely," Jarrid said, his eyes catching Becky's as she crossed her fingers for him. "Tell me the date and time, and I'll drive up to Santa Barbara."

"Let me check my appointment book and call you on that," Mr. Harrison said. "By the way, Jarrid, if I hire you, I have several associates in Santa Barbara who may be interested in corporate video and audio systems for their businesses."

Jarrid felt like it was Christmas. The second the Harrisons left his store, he lifted Becky off the floor and whirled her around the room.

"Becky, do you know what that means?"

She giggled as he spun her around. "Your dream store!" she said breathlessly. "It's going to happen, Jarrid! I know it is!"

When he set her on her feet, his hands remained on her small waist. Before he told her about his family's invitation, he had a surprise for her. A surprise he'd been planning for the past couple of days.

"I want to show you something." He took her by the hand.

"What?" she asked. "Tell me!"

"You'll see."

Jarrid locked the front door and pulled down the shades on all of the windows. Then he led her to the back of the store to his tiny office. He lit the rose-scented candle he'd bought, put on a special CD and took out two flute wineglasses and a bottle of champagne.

Becky's eyes widened with delight. ''Are we celebrating your business success?''

''Much more than that,'' Jarrid went on. ''Today's very special to us, Becky.''

He knew she would remember. Today was the date that tied their high school past, their present and hopefully their future together.

Six

Becky suddenly felt a streak of panic. The way Jarrid said "special" made her realize that it was an event involving his past with her sister. A past she didn't belong to.

"Wait, I know it'll come to me," she said, searching her mind, trying to recall the pages in her twin's diary.

"Becky, don't you remember?" Jarrid asked in a disappointed voice. "We met ten years ago today."

"Of course," she forced out. "Our ten-year anniversary. I'm so dumb!"

As he handed her a glass of champagne, her eyes misted, and she stared at the bubbles in her glass. She felt invisible to Jarrid. No matter how many customers she got for him, no matter what she did to please him, Jarrid saw her twin, not her.

"To our being together," he said.

"To us," she whispered.

Her hand trembled as she tapped his glass and sipped

the champagne. She heard a love ballad resonate through the store.

Jarrid put down her glass and gently drew her into his arms.

"Every time I play this song, I think of you," he whispered against her hair. "It was our favorite, remember?"

Her heart ached. "Yes, our favorite," she whispered back, wishing it really was, wishing she had a past, present and future with him.

The love lyrics filtered through her head as if they were being sung to her and Jarrid. She leaned her head against his shoulder as she swayed with him. Couldn't she fantasize for just a few moments that she really was her sister?

He pressed his lips to her earlobe, and tingles flittered down her body. His mouth covered hers. She parted her lips, eager to feel his tongue against hers.

As she felt him slowly unbutton her blouse and spread the fabric away from her lace-covered breasts, she knew she should leave. But the love song had entered her heart, and she yearned for him to know her more intimately.

Her bra clasp snapped open, and her skin instantly ignited as he squeezed her bare breasts with his large hands.

"Jarrid, I love when you touch me," she murmured without thinking.

"You turn me on, Becky, you really turn me on," he responded.

He took her nipple into his mouth and sucked gently. She moaned and grasped his curly hair, pushing her breast deeper into his mouth, feeling an urgency to let Jarrid know her in a way no man ever had before.

Becky wanted to forget who she really was. She wanted to be her sister completely—bold, carefree and totally Jarrid's.

She slid her hands down his rock-solid chest and touched the waistline of his pants. Then she dared to slide her palms lower and press against the zipper, feeling his growing maleness.

Jarrid groaned at her caress and expanded even larger against her hand. Her breathing was out of control. Her eyes were closed, and she slowly began to unzip his pants, desiring to touch his most private spot.

In the background of her mind, she heard the ringing of a telephone. But she was so immersed in him that she forgot where she was.

However, the persistent ringing broke through her consciousness. Her eyes popped open, realizing she was at Jarrid's store. She withdrew her fingers from his zipper and slipped free of his arms.

"You better get the phone," she said, reclasping her bra and buttoning her blouse.

As he reached for the phone on his desk, she hurried out of the tiny office to the front. Her body ached for more of his love touch. She yearned to caress him even more daringly.

Shadowy guilt filled her. If the phone hadn't rung and interrupted their heated embrace, would she have made love to Jarrid right then and there?

The answer "yes" roared through her head like a tidal wave of conflict.

In his office, Jarrid tried to listen to the customer talking to him over the phone. He could see Becky standing at the front of the store. She had her purse in her hand. A heavy feeling rushed through him. Had he overstepped his boundary again?

He tried to concentrate on his customer who was upset because he was going to give a party tomorrow night and couldn't get his new amplifier to work. He asked if Jarrid could come over tomorrow to fix it.

Jarrid reassured him that he would be there first thing in the morning. Then he hung up the phone.

"Jarrid, I better get going," Becky said. "I have a late appointment tonight to style a client's hair."

"Yeah, sure," he said. "I'll walk you to your car."

As he opened the door to his store, he wasn't sure what she was feeling. He slipped his arm around her shoulders, silently letting her know that he felt very close to her.

She leaned her head against him, and he knew that she still felt inwardly connected with him. He was sure it was the right moment to draw her deeper into his life.

When he reached her car, he couldn't wait a second longer.

"Becky, my brother and sister-in-law asked us to dinner on Sunday," he began. "Can I tell them we'll be there?"

Becky felt the momentous impact of Jarrid's words.

"You want to introduce me to your family?"

"It's about time they met the woman in my life."

Her stomach tightened. She couldn't meet his family. How could she pretend to be someone she wasn't with them?

"Jarrid, maybe we should wait."

"For what?"

For my sister to get to Los Angeles!

"What if they don't like me, Jarrid?"

"Impossible," he said. "My family will welcome you right in."

She opened her car door, positive that her sister would want her to go.

"Tell them yes," she said. "I'd love to meet them."

"All right!" he happily said, kissing her before she left.

Late that night, Becky got home from the salon and immediately dialed her twin. She needed Pam's advice on how she should act when she met Jarrid's family.

Her sister's telephone rang and rang, and before the answering machine went on, she hung up, almost relieved that her twin wasn't home.

She didn't want Pam to detect the thrilling joy she felt about meeting Jarrid's family. She was sure he was on the verge of asking her to marry him.

In bed that night she held the pillow close to her as if she was hugging Jarrid. She imagined sleeping in bed with him every night, waking up every morning with him cuddled up to her side. She knew she was dreaming, but she didn't care. He wanted to introduce her to his family!

During her lunch break, Becky went with Sherry to a café in Beverly Hills. She was too nervous to eat her turkey sandwich.

"Sherry, when you first met your in-laws," she began, "did they immediately like you?"

"My mother-in-law thought I was too skinny," Sherry replied. "My father-in-law complained that I was quieter than an ant. Other than that, they took me under their wings like their own family and haven't let me go since." She smiled knowingly. "Why? Has Jarrid invited you to meet his family?"

She nodded. "I'm so nervous about it!"

"You're glowing like an almost-engaged woman," Sherry said.

"I am?" She touched her burning cheeks.

Engaged. She loved the sound of that word related to her and Jarrid. Yes, she knew she was fantasizing again, but she couldn't help it.

"Sherry, what advice can you give me?" Becky asked. "What should I say when I meet them? How should I act?"

"Just be yourself," her friend replied. "If you pretend to be somebody you're not, they'll see right through your act and think you're a phony."

Her stomach started to ache. How could she be herself with his family when she was supposed to be her twin?

"What if they don't like me, Sherry?" she anxiously asked.

"Don't worry," her friend said reassuredly. "They're going to love you. You and Jarrid are an impeccably matched couple, that's why."

Becky took a bite out of her sandwich, unable to taste a thing. She couldn't tell Sherry the real reason she was so nervous. She was afraid that meeting Jarrid's family would attach her heart to his even more.

With Becky at his side, Jarrid parked his van in front of his brother's white stucco two-story house. His nervous system was on "overwhelm" worrying about Kenny's and Marie's reactions to her.

"Uncle Jarrid!" he heard Lizzy's voice call out.

As he got out of the van with Becky, he saw his bubbly, curly headed niece bounce her way over. Her brown eyes widened with curiosity as she stared at Becky.

"Lizzy, I want you to meet Becky Lawson," Jarrid said proudly.

Becky shook Lizzy's hand. "It's a pleasure to meet you, Lizzy."

His niece tilted her head, studying Becky. "I think you might be just right for my Uncle Jarrid, but I need to ask you one question."

"Sure, anything, Lizzy."

"If my uncle burned your cheeseburger and spilled mustard on you, would you still like him?"

"Lizzy—" Jarrid rolled his eyes, remembering his horrendous experience with Marie's friend.

"Actually, Lizzy," Becky began, "I enjoy barbecued chicken with pink lemonade. Is that okay?"

"Excellent!" Lizzy responded, her eyes twinkling with

delight. "I think you may be the woman for my Uncle Jarrid!"

As his niece led her into the house, Becky glanced back at him. "I like your family already!"

He grinned and touched the sleek angle of her back, loving her more than he could ever put into words.

The moment he saw his brother and sister-in-law waiting in the living room, his insecurity rushed to the surface. His family's eyes were intensely focused on Becky, and he could tell that Marie was carefully scrutinizing her.

Becky shook his brother's hand. "You know, you and Jarrid look very much alike."

Kenny feigned a disgusted face. "Becky, did you have to spoil my evening?"

"My brother will be on your case all night for that one, Becky," he told her kiddingly.

He felt half-relieved because he knew Kenny liked her; otherwise, he would never fool around with her.

Marie extended her hand. "It's nice to meet you, Becky," she said. "Why don't I show you around our house."

Jarrid's muscles tensed picturing Marie getting Becky alone and hurling questions at her to reveal just how serious she was about him.

"Mommy, can I show Becky my room first?" Lizzy cut in.

"Lizzy, that's a super idea!" Jarrid quickly said.

When Marie nodded, Lizzy darted up the stairs with Becky laughing close behind.

His sister-in-law turned to him with suspicious eyes.

"You *wanted* Lizzy to steal Becky from me, didn't you?"

"Well, yeah," he replied.

"I'm going to talk to her, Jarrid."

"Marie, promise you won't put any pressure on her,"

he said. "I don't want her feeling like my family's the CIA and FBI combined."

"If Becky is genuinely interested in you, why would she mind my asking a few innocent questions?"

"What kind of questions?" he asked, feeling more and more anxious by the second.

Marie mischievously grinned. "That's only for Becky and me to know." Then she disappeared into the kitchen.

Jarrid helplessly turned to his brother. "Kenny, can't you talk to your wife?"

"Marie's got her own mind set, and that's it," he replied.

"I don't want her scaring Becky off."

"What're you worried about?" his brother said. "The woman's wildly in love with you."

"You're just saying that."

"No, I'm not. I saw the way she looked at you."

"How?"

"She was all starry-eyed as if she was saying," his brother went into a high-pitched voice, "Jarrid, oh, Jarrid, you're such a hunk!"

"Kenny, don't kid me."

His brother slapped him on the back. "Come on, where's your self-confidence?"

"I want everything to go right this time," he told him. "I don't want to lose her. I love her, Kenny."

"Stop, stop!" his brother told him. "You're burning a hole in my carpet!"

"Lizzy, your room is so cool!" Becky excitedly said as she sat cross-legged, with her shoes off, on the lavender bedspread. She squeezed the nose of Lizzy's stuffed lion.

She felt cozy and comfortable in Jarrid's brother's home, as though she'd known his family for eons.

Lizzy busily searched through a box in her closet. "I found it, Becky!" she said excitedly.

She handed her a small rainbow stone.

"Becky, I want you to have this quartz crystal from my stone collection," she told her. "It's magical."

The crystal glittered in her palm. "Oh, no, I couldn't, Lizzy."

"Please take it," she insisted. "It'll bring you luck with my Uncle Jarrid."

Becky held the precious stone in her hand. "It will?" How she wished it could!

Lizzy went to her bedroom door, glanced out to make sure no one was there and then closed it.

"If I tell you a secret, will you promise not to tell Uncle Jarrid?"

She smiled. "Yes, I promise."

"I heard him talking to my mom and dad about you," she whispered. "I think he likes you a whole, whole lot."

She leaned her elbows on her knees. "Really?"

"But he's afraid of messing up," she added. "He thinks you'll change your mind and leave him."

She swallowed. "Your uncle is very, very special to me."

"Good," Lizzy said. "Because I like you a lot, too!"

Becky couldn't resist touching her button nose. "I can see why your Uncle Jarrid loves you."

Just then there was a knock on Lizzy's door. Jarrid peeked inside, and his eyes caught hers like an embrace, sending a warmth through her body.

"Lizzy, are you and Becky becoming good friends?" he asked.

"Yes, Uncle Jarrid!" Lizzy said. "Becky and I have a secret, too."

"You do? Do I get to share in it?"

Before Lizzy could respond, Marie called out, "Lizzy, can you come downstairs and set the table?"

"Okay, Mom!" Lizzy turned to Becky and whispered, "Remember, the magic works!"

"I won't forget," she whispered back. As she slipped the quartz crystal in her bag, she felt a precious closeness to Lizzy as if Lizzy were her own niece.

As Lizzy ran downstairs, Jarrid sat down on the bed beside Becky. She was very conscious of his warm, manly body close to hers. He slipped his arm around her waist and pulled her snugly against him.

"What secret was Lizzy talking about?" he asked.

"I can't tell you," she replied. "It's between your niece and me."

"Oh, yeah?" he said, his eyebrow arching. "What other secrets are you keeping from me?"

A dark shadow suddenly clouded the happiness she was feeling.

"A woman has lots of secrets," she said, glancing away.

"Tell me one."

How could she tell him she wasn't who he thought she was?

"Someday, maybe I will," she replied, knowing that dreaded day was looming up faster than she wanted.

"Jarrid, Becky, dinner's ready!" his brother called from downstairs.

"Coming!" Jarrid yelled back.

He slipped her shoes onto her feet like the prince in Cinderella, helped her up from the bed and gathered her into his arms.

"I don't care how many secrets you keep from me, Becky," he said. "As long as you're with me, I'm a happy man."

As he touched her lips with his, Becky felt a burning pain in her heart that wouldn't go away.

In the dining room Jarrid purposely kept the conversation on topics other than his past with Becky. He even began to relax a little, especially when Marie lavished Becky's plate with slices of the leg of lamb she'd specially cooked, while his brother filled her glass with vintage red wine.

Jarrid grabbed Becky's hand under the table, squeezing tightly, silently letting her know that he loved her being with him. As the dinner neared its end, he felt a ton of relief knowing all went smoothly.

Just as he and his brother helped clear the table after dessert, Marie said, "While you guys clean up, we're going for a walk."

"Who?" Jarrid asked, suddenly uneasy.

"Becky, Lizzy and I," his sister-in-law replied. "Is that all right with you?"

It wasn't at all okay, but he glanced at Becky laughing and talking to Lizzy at the front door, and he knew he couldn't interfere.

"Enjoy your walk," he said, with some trepidation.

As he anxiously watched the front door close, he felt Marie's great-grandmother's crystal bowl slipping out of his hands. His heart seemed to stop as he frantically caught the crystal within one millimeter of crashing to the floor.

His older brother threw up his hands in exasperation.

Becky strolled with Marie along the neighborhood tree-lined street, and Lizzy in-line skated on the sidewalk in front of them.

Becky's hands were clammy. Her toes felt cold inside her shoes even though it was a temperate evening.

Since the moment she had arrived at their house, she sensed that Marie was anxious to talk to her. She was scared out of her head that she might ask a question that only her twin could answer. Then Marie would find out she was a phony.

"I bet you're waiting for me to bombard you with questions," Marie began, reading her mind.

"As a matter of fact—"

"Okay, I admit it," Marie continued. "I'm overly protective of Jarrid. He's my husband's only brother, and neither of us wants to see him devastated the way he was years ago."

"Marie, I'm sorry for what happened back then," she said, struggling. "If I could go back in time and undo the pain he went through—"

Marie stopped walking and looked at her. "Becky, why did you come back into Jarrid's life?"

Her heart suddenly felt exposed. "Because I can't live without him," she confessed. "Being with Jarrid is everything to me, Marie. There's nowhere else I want to be but with him."

Her hands were suddenly trembling, and she clasped them together. Every word from her mouth was true, not because she was saying it for her sister, but from the depths of her own heart.

Marie smiled. "You know, Becky, I was hoping you'd say that."

Just then Lizzy made a full-circle turn on her blades and looked at Becky for approval. "Did you see that turn, Becky?" she asked excitedly.

"You're a professional!" Becky called out.

Lizzy beamed. "Thanks, Becky!" Then she hurried ahead on her blades.

"My daughter's growing attached to you already," Marie said. "Now you can't leave the Browning family, or else!"

The meaning of her words bit hard into Becky. She barely remembered returning to the house. She felt tormented with a mixture of overwhelming joy that Jarrid's family accepted her and an aching heart knowing she was only temporarily in their life.

In the living room, Becky found Jarrid waiting for her.

"So?" he asked. "Did Marie give you the Browning interrogation?"

"All twenty questions, right, Marie?" she asked, inwardly struggling with the warm connection she now had with Marie, almost like they really were sisters-in-law.

"Jarrid, you can relax," Marie replied. "Becky passed my test with straight A's!"

Lizzy was suddenly by Becky's side. "Becky, when can you come back again?"

Before she could answer, Marie said, "Actually, Ken and I were going to ask Jarrid to baby-sit Lizzy next Sunday afternoon while he and I go to a friend's surprise birthday party. I'm sure Lizzy would love for you to baby-sit, too, Becky."

"Will you, Becky, will you?" Lizzy asked.

She glanced at Jarrid, who had a hopeful glint in his eye.

"Sure, Lizzy, I can't wait," she replied, feeling blanketed with love from his family. A love she wasn't ready to give up.

Lizzy pulled Becky down to her size and whispered in her ear, "Don't forget to keep the lucky quartz crystal with you all the time. It works!"

"I promise," she whispered back, wishing Lizzy's dreams of her and Jarrid staying together forever could really come true.

Later, in his van, Jarrid wasn't ready to take Becky home yet. He felt rejuvenated that his family had seen what he knew all along. Becky was the one for him.

He glanced over at her in the flashing car headlights. The top buttons of her dress were slightly open. He could see the shadow of her cleavage. He wanted to hold her, touch her.

He parked his van on Mulholland Drive, overlooking the sparkling evening lights of the San Fernando Valley with the silver half-moon glowing above.

He leaned his arm on the seat behind her. He yearned to tell her how much he loved her and that he wanted to become a family with her just like Kenny, Marie and Lizzy. But he needed to know for sure if she felt that way, too.

"I envy Kenny," he began.

"Why?" Becky asked, her eyes illuminated by the sparkling city lights.

"Someday, I'd like a family just like he has." He hesitated. "Would you, Becky?"

His heart hammered against his ribs as he waited for her response. She stared out the van window at the shimmering city below. He wondered why she wasn't answering right away. If she dreamed of starting a family with him like he did with her, wouldn't she immediately say yes?

His mind was reeling. He didn't want to hang from a string anymore.

"Becky, I want to be with you," he said. "If you don't feel the same way—"

"Jarrid, I want to be with you more than with any man I've ever known, but—"

He felt like his chest was caving in. "But what, Becky?"

Her eyes were misty as she looked at him. "No buts, Jarrid." She ever so gently touched his thigh. "Tonight meant a lot to me. Your family made me feel so loved."

Her fingers felt electrical on his leg. "You are loved, Becky," he said, wanting to say more but knowing she might draw away if he let his powerful emotions take control.

He started up the van to drive her home. Her hand was still on his leg. He could barely think about the road in front of him. She hadn't said the words he'd hoped to hear about wanting to have his children, but he saw the warm love in her eyes when she looked at him. There was no way he could doubt his instincts.

He knew that sharing his family had brought her closer to him. Now he wanted to become more a part of her life.

Somehow, someway, he was determined to enter her private world, just like he'd let her into his. He wanted to show her that he could fit into her personal life as perfectly as she did in his.

Becky's telephone was ringing when she got into her apartment. She threw down her bag and picked up the phone in the living room. She was still feeling shaky, not only from her emotional visit with Jarrid's family, but from his questions about having his children, and being in his arms on Mulholland Drive.

"Beck, I've been trying to get you for hours," her twin said over the phone.

She sat down on the sofa to steady herself. "Pam, you've got to listen to me," she began. "You need to move to L.A. next week—this weekend—tomorrow!"

"Did Jarrid ask you to marry him?" her sister asked, her voice rising with hopeful anticipation.

"He's on the verge," she said.

She quickly told her sister about meeting Jarrid's family and how serious the relationship with him was getting.

"That's great!" Pam exclaimed.

"No it's not!"

"Why?"

Because I'm in love with him, she wanted to cry out.

"You need to be here, Pam." She couldn't bear his proposing to her, knowing she would not be the woman walking down the aisle with him.

"Beck, I need to tell you something." Her sister hesitated. "I've got to postpone my move to L.A."

Becky's heartbeat momentarily halted. "What?"

"My company begged me to work on a very important Japanese advertising account before I leave," her sister explained. "I might even have to go to Japan for a few days with the new male account exec I'm training to take my place. He's an incredible guy, Beck. So smart. So—"

"What about your schedule with Charlotte?" she cut in.

"Don't worry, I called Charlotte about the delay," her sister hurried on. "She said the timing was perfect because she desperately needs a vacation and plans to go to Hawaii for a couple of weeks."

Her mind was swirling in every direction. "What am I supposed to do about Jarrid?"

"Beck, I have no right to ask you to continue seeing him," her twin continued. "If you want to stop my whole silly plan right now, I wouldn't blame you."

Becky jumped off the sofa. "Stop seeing Jarrid?"

"I've asked so much of you already," Pam went on. "You're probably tired of being with him."

"No, no, I like spending time with him," she blurted out and then quickly added, "I mean, for you."

"Then you won't mind pretending to be me for a little while longer?" her twin asked. "I mean, even though he's getting really serious?"

Oh, Pam, I can't keep myself away from him! "I'll continue seeing him until you get here," she promised.

"Somehow, I'll pay you back, sis," Pam said. "I promise."

In a turmoil, Becky hung up. Her forehead ached. Her lower back throbbed with tension. She needed a hot bath. She needed an aspirin. She needed Jarrid.

Her sister had offered her an out, but she couldn't take it. Her twin could've called Jarrid from New York, explained the entire situation and seen him when she arrived in Los Angeles.

However, Becky couldn't imagine abruptly ending her relationship with Jarrid. She had promised to baby-sit Lizzy with him on Sunday. She needed to help him get that job designing the home theater for the Harrisons' Santa Barbara house. She needed to—

She was totally enveloped in his life!

Feeling in a frenzy, she realized she was pacing back and forth in her living room. She had to quell the avalanche of intimate emotions she felt for Jarrid. She had to! But how?

The next afternoon Jarrid parked his van at a meter in front of the salon. He glanced at his watch. He was expected at Mrs. Fuller's house to install a carousel CD player and videotape machine. Of course, Mrs. Fuller had also insisted that he take advantage of her Jacuzzi and pool afterward.

However, Jarrid couldn't think about work. He had to see Becky first. He got out of his van. He realized that she'd dropped by his store several times. Yet she'd never invited him inside the salon to share her job.

He was determined to become more of a part of her life now, even if he had to take the initiative himself.

When Jarrid opened the glass door of the salon, he was hit with the sound of rock music, whirring hair dryers and pleasant chitchat. He immediately spotted Becky busily blow-drying a client's hair, but her back was to him so she didn't see him enter.

She looked like an artist as she sculpted the woman's hair with precision and concentration. He felt a spark of pride in her work. Every new thing he saw about her made him love her even more.

"Hi, Jarrid!" a somewhat familiar female voice said from behind him.

He turned to see Sherry, who was sipping a cup of coffee.

"I hope Becky doesn't mind my stopping by," he said. "She looks really busy. I don't want to interrupt her."

"Becky will be happy you came," Sherry said with a warm smile. "I hear that she met your family."

He grinned. "Yeah, she definitely won them over."

"I bet you're anxious to meet her side, too."

He looked at her. "I met Becky's mother and father before they passed away."

"You did?"

"Many years ago."

Sherry looked confused. "You and Becky knew each other before you met at the gym?"

"Sure." He hesitated. "Didn't she tell you?"

"Well, I—" Her eyes darted toward Becky as if she didn't know whether she should say any more.

Jarrid's gut tightened. Suddenly a landslide of doubts about her feelings for him returned. Why wouldn't she tell her friend they knew each other before?

Seven

Becky finished styling her client's hair and was about to open the velcro fastener of the client's smock when she looked up to see if her next customer had arrived.

Her breath was instantly knocked out of her when she saw Jarrid in the salon!

Becky didn't remember removing the smock from her client. She couldn't even recall leaving her work station and walking toward Jarrid.

In the next instant she was standing near him, praying Sherry hadn't inadvertently said anything that might destroy the little time she had left with him.

"Jarrid, what a surprise!" she said, trying to stay calm, but the troubled expression on his face immediately upset her.

"I hope it's okay that I dropped by," he said, looking tense.

"I'm really glad you came," she replied worriedly.

"Ah, Becky," Sherry began in an awkward tone. "Jarrid was just telling me that he met your parents a few years ago."

Her stomach cringed. "Yes, yes, he did," she rushed out, turning to him. "Jarrid, why don't I show you my work station."

As Jarrid walked ahead of her, she glanced back and frantically mouthed to Sherry, hoping she would forgive her, "I'll explain later."

The moment she took him to her work station, he immediately turned to her.

"Why didn't you tell Sherry that we went together years ago?"

She gulped, her thoughts chaotic. "Because I was ashamed to tell her about the pain I caused you," she replied, searching for an answer. "I wanted to forget what I did to you, Jarrid. I wanted to start anew, so I kept the past to myself."

The lies! She despised herself for not telling him that she was a fake.

When Jarrid remained quiet, tinkering with her hair-cutting tools on the counter, her worries increased.

"Jarrid, I didn't mean to offend you."

He looked up. "Becky, I can't help wondering if your feelings for me are going to change again."

"No, Jarrid, never," she told him with all her soul.

"How can I be sure?"

Before she could answer, she saw Jarrid's eyes dart to the clock on the salon wall. "Geez! I forgot all about Mrs. Fuller!"

"Do you have to leave?" Everything felt so unfinished between them.

"I'm already fifteen minutes late," he replied. "Why don't you come with me?"

She felt a rush of anxiety. "But I've got one more appointment." She wanted to go with him. She needed to make sure everything was okay between them, not just for her sister, but for herself.

Just then, Sherry reached on the counter to borrow her blow-dryer. "Becky, your next customer is a walk-in, not one of your regulars. I can take care of her."

She looked at Jarrid, knowing she had to mend the doubts she'd created in his mind.

"Give me a few minutes to clean up," she told him as she started putting away her hair-styling equipment. "I'll take my car and meet you there."

His face relaxed. "I'll call Mrs. Fuller to let her know I'm on my way and you'll be with me."

When Jarrid was out of the door, Becky felt Sherry watching her. "What's going on, Becky? Why are you so secretive about your past with Jarrid?"

She squeezed the plastic hair sprayer until it was about to burst in her hand.

"My relationship with Jarrid has gotten so complicated, Sherry," she revealed. "I want to tell you about it, but I can't just yet."

She prayed her friend would understand.

"Whenever you need to talk, I'm here," Sherry said. "I think you know how I feel, Becky. I want to see you and Jarrid end up together."

Becky felt a lump in her throat. She impulsively hugged Sherry and hurried out of the salon.

In the family room at Mrs. Fuller's house, Jarrid noticed that Becky was so tense that she couldn't even sit on the sofa. She stood by the sliding glass patio door as she talked to Mrs. Fuller while he hooked up the machines.

He still hadn't had a chance to talk to her and couldn't shake the feeling that she was going through major changes about their relationship. Why else would she be so anxious about his finding out that she'd hidden their past love from her friend?

As he connected the wires, he couldn't help wondering whether she was with him only out of guilt to make up for the turmoil she had caused him seven years ago, or because she truly loved him. His insides roared for an answer.

Just then, Jarrid heard Mrs. Fuller telling Becky that her housekeeper was off for the day and she was leaving the house. She insisted that Becky take a Jacuzzi while waiting for him to finish his work. He could see Becky hesitating, but she followed Mrs. Fuller to the guest house to put on a swimsuit.

As Jarrid tested the equipment he'd installed, he wished he could obliterate the uncertainty he felt about their relationship. If he could only believe that she truly loved him.

A few minutes later he glanced out the glass patio door and saw Becky lying on a lounge chair outside. He finished his work and walked onto the patio, ready to talk to her.

Her eyes were closed. Her strawberry hair was glimmering in the sunshine. Her rosebud lips were slightly parted. He fought the overwhelming rush of love and desire he felt for her.

His gaze traveled down her turquoise bikinied body. Her ivory breasts swelled over the skimpy top. His eyes lingered on the wisp of turquoise covering her feminine mound.

This time, he wasn't going to act on his impulses. He remembered he promised Mrs. Fuller that he would make use of her pool. Needing time to think, he went into the guest house to change into swimming trunks.

As Becky lay on the lounge chair, her skin burned hot, not just from the rays of the sun, but from feeling Jarrid gazing at her a few feet away.

She felt almost naked in her borrowed, scanty bikini.

Normally, she never would have worn such a revealing swimsuit. But with Jarrid, she felt the reserved side of herself disappear.

She got up from the lounge chair and glanced toward the guest house. She was sure he was doubting her love for him. She wished there was some way she could show him that he meant everything to her.

She stared at the still water of the pool, wanting to rev up the nerve to dive in, wishing she had the courage to ask Jarrid, straight-out, if he could ever love her knowing she wasn't her twin.

"Becky, what're you thinking about?"

She whirled around and saw Jarrid standing a few feet from her, all muscular and strong in snug, black swim trunks.

"I was wishing I wasn't afraid of—" she hesitated "—the water."

As he walked over to her, she felt her skin grow molten hot from the nearness of his half-naked body.

"Do you trust me, Becky?" he asked.

"Yes."

"Completely?"

When she nodded, he took her hand in his and led her to the edge of the pool.

She gently pulled back. "Jarrid, what're you doing?"

"I want to show you there's nothing to be afraid of— not the dark—not the water—not us."

She knew he was looking for confirmation that she loved and trusted him. She wanted to give him that, but her fear of sinking underwater and drowning was too strong.

"Jarrid, I can't go in the pool."

"I'll stay with you every second," he said. "I would never let anything happen to you, Becky."

She knew he was pledging his love to her. If she refused

to have faith in him, he would think she didn't love him in return.

Becky stuck her toe in the pool. "It's too cold."

He climbed into the five-foot depth. "Take my hand."

She hesitantly put her palm in his. "Jarrid, how can I be sure this is going to work?"

"You've got my personal guarantee," he said, then he guided her into the transparent blue.

As the cool liquid covered her thighs, tummy and breasts, the water movement gently pushed her against him, making her sharply conscious of his ruggedly sturdy body.

"Lie on your back," he said. "I won't let you sink."

Her heart was pounding as she held on to his hard-muscled arm and leaned back on the surface of the water. She felt his hands settle under her back below the water. She was acutely aware of his vital fingers firmly against her bare skin.

"Relax," he instructed. "In a second, the water will hold you up."

She felt his hands slowly slip away from her body. A streak of fear went through her as she expected her body to sink. But he was standing near her, and she knew he would never leave. She soon became aware of the weight-lessness of her body floating on top of the water, and she felt an exhilarated freedom.

In the next instant, Jarrid drew her against his solid body. "Do you feel safe, Becky?"

"Very safe," she whispered, circling her arms around his neck, wanting to be held by him forever.

Jarrid felt a rush of love for Becky. She'd trusted him completely over her fears. He knew how difficult that had been for her.

Her eyes were linked to his, open, seductive, welcoming. He was super-aware of her bikini-clad body in his arms.

Without thinking, his mouth grazed her lips, her cheeks, her neck, and then his lips found the valley of her breasts above the bikini top.

He slowly let her feet touch the concrete bottom of the pool, and then he crushed her ample curves against his chest. As he hungrily kissed her, he felt her responding with equal fervor.

He was immersed in her. Nothing else existed. Just Becky. Just the woman he loved.

He undid her bikini top. His mouth found her bare breast, and he licked and suckled her nipple. She moaned as he nibbled on her taut tip until it was swollen from his tongue's caress.

His hand drifted down her belly, and he heard her gasp when he reached the crevice between her thighs. Sparks of desire exploded through him as he stroked her pleasure area. He felt her hands grip his bare back as he quickened his strokes on her fabric-covered womanhood.

His rock-hard manhood grew huge against her thigh, wanting her, desiring her completely. He felt her hands slide down his back and reach the elastic of his swim trunks.

He held his breath as she slipped her fingers inside the back of his swimsuit and grasped his bare buttocks. His masculinity swelled, straining against the spandex.

Just as he was about to slip his finger underneath the patch of bikini, Becky slowly drew away from him.

"Jarrid, it—it's late," she stammered. "I need to get home."

Without another word, she hurried out of the pool, clutching her bikini top, and ran into the guest house.

Every blood vessel in Jarrid's body was ready to burst, not just from desire for her, but from frustration with himself. She trusted him totally, but he couldn't restrain his need for her. He couldn't keep the promise he'd made to himself not to act on impulse with her.

Frustrated, he climbed out of the pool and dried off with a towel. Realizing the time, he went into the house to find the phone. He was so consumed with Becky that he had neglected to return to the store at the time he told Pete he would.

As he dialed and waited for Pete to answer, he worried that he was rushing her and might once again push her out of his life.

"Pete," he said when he heard his technician's voice. "Sorry, but I got delayed."

"Mr. Harrison called a couple of minutes ago," Pete replied.

"Did he leave a message?" He was angry with himself. He'd been expecting Mr. Harrison's call and should've been at the store to talk to him.

"He said he'll be out of town for a couple of days," his technician replied. "He'll call you when he returns."

He felt like slamming his fist against a wall. If he'd been at the store like he was supposed to, he would've set a definite appointment to drive to Santa Barbara for their meeting. Now he had to hope that Mr. Harrison would call back.

As Pete began telling him about other business matters at the store, Jarrid glanced toward the guest house. His intense longing for Becky was affecting his entire life. He had to ease up on his relationship with her. But how could he? Not only was his personal life entwined with her, but now his business life was, as well.

In the guest house, Becky's hands trembled as she brushed her wet hair. Her skin was still on fire from caressing Jarrid's aroused body. She couldn't believe how risqué she'd been in the pool with him. She had wanted to touch him in ways that a woman did only with the man she was going to marry.

As she blindly stuffed her hairbrush into her bag, she knocked her finger against Lizzy's quartz crystal. She gently squeezed the stone in her hand, wishing Jarrid could be her man, fantasizing that her sister wouldn't be able to move to Los Angeles, and she would be with him for always.

Her line of thinking paralyzed her. How could she even consider not wanting her sister to come to L.A.? How could she so easily throw away her dream of being a close family with her twin?

She knew why. Because in the pool, she felt magical being in Jarrid's arms. She felt sensual, venturesome, bold and incredibly loved by him. And she wanted more, so much more of him.

She quickly put the crystal back in her bag, trying to quiet her throbbing heart, steaming body and guilty conscience.

As she left the guest house, she saw Jarrid standing in the living room on the telephone. A towel was wrapped low around his waist. He nervously ran his fingers through his wet hair.

She knew he was emotionally struggling about her pulling away from him at the pool. She wanted to tell him that she ached to make passionate love to him but could never fulfill her desire.

Instead she hurried off Mrs. Fuller's property before he saw her.

On Sunday at his brother's house, Jarrid nervously glanced at his watch as he waited for Lizzy to get ready for his day with her.

He hoped Becky remembered. He hadn't called her since their caresses in the pool. He was trying to get more involved in his own life and not need her so badly. It had taken all of his willpower not to pick up the phone or go over to see her.

"So, Jarrid?" Kenny asked, all dressed up for his friend's surprise birthday party. "Have you hurled the ultimate question at Becky?"

Jarrid shifted uneasily. "Not yet."

"What's the delay?" his brother pushed. "Are you waiting for her to propose first?"

"I need time, Kenny."

"You're putting it off."

"No I'm not."

"Yes you are," his brother insisted. "You're afraid she's going to double reject you."

He shoved his hands deep into his jeans pockets. "Okay, so I am."

"Marie thinks Becky will say yes the moment you ask her."

He stared at Kenny. "Did Becky tell her that?"

"Not directly."

"Then Marie doesn't know for sure."

"If you're waiting for a written guarantee beforehand—"

"Uncle Jarrid, come on, let's go pick up Becky!"

Lizzy grabbed his hand and led him out of the house before he could deal with his brother's stinging, on-the-bull's-eye comment.

At the Los Angeles Zoo, Becky held Lizzy's and Jarrid's hands as they walked together past the pink flamingos. She inwardly fought the feeling that the three of them were like a family.

However, as Lizzy skipped next to her, and Jarrid squeezed her hand, she was losing the battle.

"Becky, you know what I wish?" Lizzy began.

"What, Lizzy?"

"I wish you were my aunt."

Becky swallowed, glancing at Jarrid. "You know, Lizzy, that's a very big wish."

"I know, but saying 'Aunt Becky' sounds so good to me!" Lizzy went on. "Why can't it come true? You're the best lady my Uncle Jarrid's ever been with."

"Lizzy, I think you're putting Becky on the spot," Jarrid said uncomfortably.

"It's okay," Becky told him.

But it wasn't okay. She wanted more than anything to be in the Browning family.

"Lizzy, becoming your aunt would be a very complicated process."

"Why?" she asked. "Uncle Jarrid loves you and you love Uncle Jarrid so—"

Just then, Lizzy's attention was interrupted by the ringing of a bell on a cotton candy cart.

"Oh, cotton candy, my favorite!" Lizzy said excitedly.

Jarrid handed her a few dollars. "Buy one for Becky, too."

As Lizzy happily skipped over to the candy cart, Jarrid watched Becky walk over to the giant turtles in the pond. He fought the disappointment rising within him.

Becky never really answered Lizzy's aunt question. He wanted to hear her say, "Lizzy, I'll be your aunt the second your uncle proposes."

But she didn't. He wondered if she would ever be ready to marry him.

His brother's written-guarantee comment bellowed through his brain. Maybe he was so nervous about making a second marriage proposal to her that he was overblowing everything she said and did.

He walked over to Becky and slipped his arm around her

waist. "I hope Lizzy's curious question didn't spoil your time with us."

"Oh, no," she replied. "I'm having a great time with the two of you."

As Lizzy hurried back and handed Becky a puff of pink cotton candy, he chided himself for overreacting to every little thing she said. His brother was right. He was putting off what he wanted to do more than anything in his life. He had to figure out a way to ask Becky to marry him that wouldn't invite the answer no.

Being with Jarrid and Lizzy at the zoo went by too quickly for Becky. As she sat next to him in the front seat of his van with Lizzy in the back seat, she wanted to hold on to the fantasy that Jarrid was her husband and Lizzy was their daughter for just a little while longer.

Just as Becky was about to get out of the van, in front of her apartment building, Lizzy whispered in her ear, "I *still* wish you were my aunt! And my biggest wishes *always* come true!"

Becky gave her a kiss on the cheek. "Lizzy, you're the sweetest niece an aunt could ever want," she whispered, knowing she would give anything to be her aunt and part of Jarrid's family.

As Lizzy waited in the van, Jarrid walked her to her apartment. The sadness she felt was overwhelming. She had to spend less time with him. She had to.

She was about to put the key in the lock when he took her hand in his.

"Will you have dinner with me at my apartment Tuesday night?" he asked.

She almost dropped her apartment key. Alone with him at his apartment? In the intimacy of his home? She couldn't!

"Jarrid, I might have late appointments that night."

"Say yes, Becky," he persisted. "I want to show you my place. I promise not to cook sushi."

She couldn't help but smile, remembering her first evening getting to know him. Now she knew him in ways she never dreamed of. Ways that made her fall wildly in love with him.

She began to open her apartment door, struggling with how to tell him she couldn't. Suddenly she heard her twin's voice on the answering machine saying, "Hi, Beck, just wanted to check in. I'm going out, so don't call me—"

Panicking, she burst out, "Yes, sure, dinner at your apartment, definitely."

Then she hurried into her apartment and closed the door before he heard any more.

Back at his van, Jarrid found Lizzy listening to an easy-rock station on the radio.

"You know, Uncle Jarrid," she began. "I think you need some coaching."

He looked at her, surprised. "Coaching on what?"

"How to ask Becky to marry you."

He raised an eyebrow. "Exactly what do you know about that topic?"

"I'm no expert," she continued, "but it seems to me that you're a chicken about it."

"Oh, yeah?" Were his doubts about himself so obvious that even his niece was aware of it?

Lizzy lowered the radio. "You've gotta take Becky to a small café and order a cappuccino with a delicious pastry. That's what my dad does when my mom is mad at him and he wants her to be in love with him again."

He started up the van and headed toward his brother's house. "I see. Go on."

Lizzy straightened in her seat. "At the café, you take Becky's hand," she went on, "slide the big, big diamond ring on her finger and zip out the question, 'Becky, will you be my honey forever?' It's simple. I saw it on television once.''

He parked in front of her house. ''What if Becky says no?'' His stomach churned just thinking about her rejecting him a second time.

Lizzy opened the van door. ''Uncle Jarrid, just follow my lines, okay? Becky's waiting for you to ask her.'' Then she gave him a big kiss on the cheek and hurried toward the front door of her house, where her mother and father were waiting for her.

Kenny and Marie waved to him as he drove off. He couldn't believe it. A nine-year-old was giving him advice on how to propose to the woman he loved because he didn't have the nerve to do it himself!

Jarrid pushed his foot down hard on the accelerator. He knew one thing for sure. He couldn't monkey around anymore. He had to find the most romantic of moments and just blurt out the question, ''Becky, will you marry me?'' Yes! Simple!

Jarrid confidently parked his van, got out and slammed the locked door closed. Nothing to get worried about. Then how come he'd just locked his keys in the van thinking about it?

Eight

On Tuesday afternoon at the salon, Becky was so nervous about going to Jarrid's apartment that she was about to apply platinum blond hair dye on a client who asked for jet black.

She quickly corrected her near mistake, and after finishing, she escaped into the coffee room to regain her equilibrium. She had to call Jarrid and tell him she was overwhelmed with appointments and couldn't come.

She was just about to pick up the phone to dial his store number when Sherry walked into the coffee room. In her hand was a bouquet of fragrant white gardenias sprinkled with baby's breath.

"Becky, these flowers were just delivered for you," Sherry said.

"For me?" No one had ever hand-delivered flowers to her before.

"I bet I know who they're from," her friend said.

She sucked in her breath as she held the fragrant bouquet in her hand and opened the card. "Been thinking about you all morning. Can't wait to see you for dinner at my place tonight. Jarrid."

"He's so in love with you," Sherry said. "Obviously, your going to his apartment means a lot to him."

Becky smelled the scented gardenias, feeling more anxious than ever. She knew if she canceled out he'd be very hurt. She could never do that to him.

"Sherry, what should I do when I get there?" she nervously asked. "Offer to help him cook?"

"Cook?" her friend repeated incredulously. "Becky, tonight could be the most intimate evening of your relationship with him. You may not even make it to the dinner table."

"Sherry, don't say that!" she rushed out, putting the flowers into a vase, knowing her friend was verbalizing her greatest desire.

Sherry studied her. "Why are you holding back your love for Jarrid?"

The words flew out before she realized it. "Because I'll never end up with him, Sherry."

Just then, Becky's next client arrived to have her hair done. She felt torn inside. She needed to share her dilemma with Sherry. She wanted to hear her opinion, but she knew she couldn't say another word.

"Becky, I don't know what's going on with you," Sherry said. "But I'm positive about one thing. Jarrid Browning is the man you're going to marry."

Becky's lower back ached with tension as she snipped, cut and curled her next client's hair. She had to settle her nerves before she went to Jarrid's apartment. She had to force herself to put Jarrid out of her mind for the rest of her workday.

However, the more she tried, Jarrid's smile, his electric

touch, his manly scent, everything about him permeated her every thought.

In the late afternoon, she glanced at the clock, realizing she only had one hour to get ready to go to his apartment.

She grabbed her bag, reached for the vase and handed Sherry one perfect white gardenia. "Thanks for being my guardian angel." Then she hurried home.

At his apartment, Jarrid fried up his specialty breaded chicken in a pan, took a quick taste of the garlic potatoes baking in the oven and hurled the red leaf lettuce into a bowl to prepare the mixed green salad.

There was no doubt about it. He wanted to make Becky feel so at home at his place that when he finally asked her to marry him she would say yes ten times over. He hoped the gardenias he sent had expressed his love and thoughts of a future with her.

As he cut up tomatoes for the salad, Jarrid smiled thinking about Mr. Harrison's call a few hours ago at the store. An appointment had been set up for next weekend, to meet at his Santa Barbara house. He wanted Jarrid to sample sketch an extensive home theater system.

Jarrid popped a crouton in his mouth. He had a good feeling about getting that job. He was on his way to expanding his business.

He began pouring a bottle of Caesar salad dressing on the lettuce. His luck had sped uphill the moment he'd reconnected with Becky. He almost felt like his home entertainment store was "their" store. He pictured the neon sign above his store reading, "Jarrid & Becky Browning Home Entertainment Company."

Suddenly he realized that he was pouring the entire bottle of Caesar dressing into the bowl, and the salad was drowning in dressing!

You're in fantasy land, he told himself. The truth was

Becky had never said one syllable about spending the rest of her life with him. Yet, in his gut, he felt like she wanted to.

That's why tonight, in his private domain, he wanted her to feel so comfortable, so close to him, that when he uttered the words *wife* and *marriage,* she wouldn't hesitate for even a moment to accept his proposal.

Just then the doorbell rang. Jarrid quickly turned off the flame on the stovetop and lowered the oven temperature. As he dashed toward the front door, from the corner of his eyes, he spotted his white socks lying on the living room floor. He quickly stuffed the socks into a drawer of a cabinet.

Then he anxiously swung open the door to find the woman of his dreams standing there looking more beautiful than the last time he saw her.

All of Becky's fears and anxieties immediately melted away when her eyes met Jarrid's. He was looking at her like her presence lit up his life.

"I hope I'm not too early," she said.

"I'm glad you are," he said. "Now I've got more time to spend with you."

Why did Jarrid have to look so handsome in his cranberry button-down shirt, open at the collar, and stonewashed jeans? Did he have to make her feel so special, when she was struggling to detach her heart from his?

As she stepped into his apartment, Becky took in the hardwood floors, well-used sofa, teak coffee table piled high with magazines and newspapers, large gray throw rug and sleek black entertainment system that took up an entire wall of his living room.

"What an incredible apartment!" she said, feeling totally at home.

"Sure is—when you're in it," he said with a slow grin that made her knees feel weak.

Trying to ignore her desire to throw her arms around his neck and kiss him, she checked out his entertainment unit. "Wow, what a sound system."

When he didn't respond, she turned and caught his eyes steady on her.

"Becky, it's so great having you here."

"You better not keep saying that or I won't leave," she kidded.

"That's exactly what I'm hoping," he said, his gaze holding hers.

Her cheeks grew hot just thinking about remaining overnight with him. She had to get off that topic fast!

"What CDs do you have?"

"Jazz, rock, classical," he replied. "Pick out your favorite in one of those drawers while I get our sushi ready." He winked and left the living room.

Becky took a deep breath of air. How much longer could she conceal the utter ecstasy she felt being with him?

As she opened one of the cabinet drawers to look at his CDs, she found a pair of crumpled white socks. She smiled, figuring he hid them so she would think he wasn't messy.

She felt the sudden urge to take care of him. She wondered if he had a hamper so she could throw them in.

She glanced into the bathroom where his razor and shaving cream lay on the sink. His bath towel was hanging over the shower door. She wanted to mentally photograph every inch of his place so she'd never forget it.

Seeing no hamper, she hesitantly peeked into his bedroom. He had a walnut chest of drawers with his keys lying on top. A small television was on a stand near his bed. Her gaze landed on his double bed covered with a royal blue comforter. Her breathing quickened as she pictured Jarrid lying naked under the sheets with her bare skin pressed against his muscled body. Her breasts throbbed at the thought of making fiery love to him.

Just then she heard a loud jangle of silverware crashing to the floor in the kitchen, making her super-aware of her sensually charged thoughts about him.

"I've got everything under control!" she heard Jarrid call out.

She wished she did! Her body suddenly felt tense. The ache in her lower back returned. Why was she dreaming about Jarrid when she could never fulfill her fantasy?

She hurried back to the living room and sat on the sofa, rubbing her back with her fingertips, trying to relax. She knew she couldn't stay at his apartment for very long or she would give in to her desires.

"Becky, did you strain your back?" Jarrid's low voice resonated from behind her.

"I guess a little at work today," she replied.

He sat down next to her on the sofa.

"Does it hurt right here?" he asked, gently touching her back, sending a tingle up her spine.

She nodded, swallowing, feeling the warmth of his fingers through her skirt.

"Probably from standing all day at the salon," she explained, trying to steady her voice.

"You're definitely tense," he said.

She held her breath as he tenderly circled his fingers along her back.

"Lie down on the rug," he suggested. "I'll massage your muscles."

A massage? She couldn't! But before she could protest, Jarrid took her hand and helped her off the sofa. She lay down on her stomach on the soft rug. Her body trembled as she felt him straddle her and begin stroking her lower back.

"Relax," he said in a soothing, deep voice.

Her heartbeat raced as his thumbs firmly kneaded her aching back.

"It feels good," she couldn't help but utter.

"I can feel your muscles loosening up already," he said, his voice getting a bit husky.

She sucked in her breath as she felt his fingers move lower down her back. Hot blood streamed through her veins. *You're relaxed, so why aren't you ending the massage?* she silently asked herself.

She knew exactly why. She wanted his hands to remain on her body, all over her body, in fact.

Jarrid's pulse raced as he stroked Becky's muscles. His mind was filled with words of love he wanted to express to her, questions he wanted to ask about their future together.

As he kneaded her muscles, his fingers landed on the zipper of her skirt. He lowered the zipper so he could massage the muscles of her bare back.

Her naked skin felt so soft, so warm, against his fingertips. He slid down the elastic of her panties to touch more of her.

A low moan escaped from Becky's lips as he squeezed her firm flesh. As he stroked her two ivory moons, his hand slipped between the crevice of her bare thighs. She gasped as he intimately slid his finger inside her moistness.

He leaned forward, brushing his face against her hair, smelling the sweetness of her, needing her, desiring to merge his throbbing body with hers.

"Becky," Jarrid murmured. "I want you so much."

He thought he heard her whisper, "Jarrid, I want you, too."

He felt her spasm as his finger moved inside of her. His manhood pushed against his jeans, wanting to blend his entire being with hers.

In the next instant, Jarrid felt Becky slipping free of his caresses. She arose from the floor. Her cheeks were flushed, her hair a little mussed and her eyes were filled with concern.

"Jarrid, I—I'm sorry," she stammered. "I just need to take it slower." Then she hurried into the bathroom.

Disappointed in himself, he went into the kitchen. He yanked open the kitchen cabinet to pull out a couple of dishes. He hadn't meant to try to make love to her.

Yet he'd sensed her need for him as strongly as his need for her. He obviously read her wrong. Couldn't he see that she wasn't ready to make love to him yet?

He anxiously looked toward the closed bathroom door, wondering what she was thinking, what she was feeling. She never told him. She kept so much to herself. He didn't understand why she wouldn't completely open up all of her thoughts and feelings to him.

In the bathroom, Becky's hand was on the doorknob, but she was hesitant to go back outside to Jarrid. She knew he was upset with her. She didn't blame him. She wanted him to intimately touch her, and he knew that. However, her desire to sexually merge with him grew so intense that she had to pull away.

She walked to the kitchen door and saw Jarrid setting down plates of fried chicken and potatoes. He had white napkins folded at each place setting. Two tall red candles sat in the middle of the small table.

Loving feelings flooded through her. She'd give up anything to be her sister so she could have Jarrid.

Jarrid caught her watching him. "Do you still want to stay for dinner?"

"Of course," she quickly replied. "I need to see what kind of cook you are."

"Becky, when I was massaging your back, I never meant to—"

"Don't explain, Jarrid," she told him. "I wanted it as much as you did. What I'm worried about is where you're hiding the sushi."

His face relaxed as he pulled out a chair for her at the table.

As she sat in his cozy kitchen eating his scrumptious chicken, she longed to share meals with him every morning, afternoon and evening, as his wife.

After she helped wash and dry the dinner dishes, Jarrid sensed that Becky was ready to leave. Asking her to marry him gnawed at his brain. He realized that the perfect opportunity was glaring him in the face.

As he walked her to her car in the evening darkness, his heart thumped against his ribs. He knew he would be stepping over the line with his invitation, but he couldn't hold back.

"Becky, I've got an early morning appointment with Mr. Harrison this Saturday at his house in Santa Barbara," he began. "Will you drive up to Santa Barbara with me on Friday night?"

His collar suddenly felt tight around his neck. Driving up on Friday for an early-morning appointment meant staying overnight in a motel room.

"Santa Barbara?" she repeated in an anxious voice.

"Don't worry," he quickly added. "I'll get us separate hotel rooms with a connecting door that locks."

"I don't know, Jarrid," she hesitantly said.

"Come with me, Becky," he persisted. "I can't go without you. If it wasn't for you, I wouldn't even have this meeting."

"I'll try," she said. "I need to check my salon appointments."

After Becky left in her car, Jarrid kept his hopes sky-high that she would go with him. Because, in the romantic setting of Santa Barbara, he planned to ask Becky to be his bride.

Becky hurriedly parked her VW Rabbit in her carport. She turned off the engine, anxious to call her sister about the invitation.

She had to convince her twin that she couldn't accompany Jarrid to Santa Barbara.

Because every inch of her was yearning to go!

She searched her bag for her apartment key. She felt torn inside. She longed to go with Jarrid, not only to encourage Mr. Harrison to hire him and make his business dream come true but also she wanted to spend an entire romantic weekend with him before her time with him was up.

She unlocked her apartment door and pushed up the light switch. The lights wouldn't go on. She frantically flicked the switch up and down, but nothing happened.

Without thinking, she barreled into the darkness straight to the kitchen to find her flashlight. Just as she reached for the flashlight, she suddenly realized that she wasn't afraid of the dark.

Jarrid Browning had altered her life forever. He'd made her see the world through his eyes. He'd touched her so deeply inside that he was already a permanent part of her.

That's why she didn't dare go to Santa Barbara with him. She was afraid that she would get so caught up being alone with him for the weekend that she wouldn't be able to resist making love to him.

Just then her apartment lights went on, and she noticed the message machine light blinking. When she quickly turned it on, her twin's voice immediately filled the room.

"Beck, I'm calling from an airplane on my way to Japan! Yes, you heard right. Japan!"

Becky's mind was spinning. *Pam, you can't do this to me!*

Her sister's excited voice went on. "The company sent me with the new account exec to complete this big account in Tokyo. I'll be gone for a few days."

She suddenly couldn't breathe. Jarrid. Santa Barbara. Connecting hotel rooms. What was she going to do?

"Beck," her sister went on, "don't worry. I'll be in L.A. soon. I know you're taking advantage of every opportunity to make my relationship with Jarrid go perfectly. I love you, sis!"

Caught in a tornado of emotion, Becky turned off the answering machine. Her sister's expectations of her loomed above her head like a ton of steel ready to fall. Once she told her sister about the connecting hotel rooms, she knew her twin would insist she go to Santa Barbara to solidify her relationship with him.

How could she say no to him now? If she refused his invitation without her sister's okay, knowing how much going to Santa Barbara meant to him, she might ruin Pam's relationship with him before she even got to L.A.

Feeling torn inside, Becky reached into her bag for Lizzy's quartz crystal. She squeezed the stone in the palm of her hand, hoping the lucky piece would give her the willpower to keep out of Jarrid's arms.

She knew she could never make love to him, no matter how much she wanted to. She had to be true to her sister. And also, making love to Jarrid would seal her soul to his forever.

Early Friday evening, driving up to Santa Barbara with Becky at his side, Jarrid felt an exhilaration that satisfied his soul. He glanced over at her. She was looking at the map, like they'd been going on trips together for years.

Find the right moment and ask her to marry you, he told himself. *No more hesitations, doubts or delays!*

His throat suddenly went dry. His hands perspired on the steering wheel. When would be the perfect time? Should he wait until they were in the hotel? How about after his meeting?

Jarrid squeezed the steering wheel tighter, trying to find the romantic words that would cause Becky to want to say yes. He nervously ran proposal phrases through his head until he couldn't think straight anymore.

"Jarrid, did you say we were staying at the Blue Sea Hotel?" Becky asked, cutting into his tension-filled thoughts.

"That's the name."

"I think we just passed it."

"We did?" He was so caught up in his worries that he didn't realize he'd already reached their destination.

When Jarrid parked his van and went to get their hotel room keys, Becky was so nervous that she was ready to tell him to immediately return her to Los Angeles. She fumbled with the door handle and got out of the van, needing to walk off her intense anxiety.

The path alongside the hotel, she realized, led to a small private beach. She could hear the waves crashing and see the white foam rush up to the shore in the darkness.

She gazed up at the stars sparkling in the black velvet sky. The half-moon glittered in the vast expanse of the cosmos.

Becky knew it was crazy, but for an instant, she felt like she was on her honeymoon with Jarrid. Just the two of them. Alone with the man she adored, for one romantic weekend.

Just then she felt Jarrid behind her. He slipped his arms around her waist and gazed up at the sparkling sky with her. "Do you want to drive to the wharf and take a walk along the pier?"

His deep voice was close to her ear. His warm breath on her cheek. His solid body pressed against her back. She could remain in his arms under the moonlight forever.

"Sounds perfect," she said.

On the Santa Barbara wharf, Becky leaned against Jarrid's shoulder as she watched the fishing boats sway back and forth at the dock. There was so much she wanted to say to him. But she kept her secret love words buried deep within her heart.

"I care about you so much, Becky," Jarrid whispered into her hair. "I can't imagine being without you."

Then his mouth touched hers, first gently and then more passionately. She parted her lips, meeting his tongue with hers, needing to show him that she cared, too. Oh, how she cared!

She tightened her arms around him and pressed her body to his. "I feel so lucky being with you, Jarrid," she couldn't help but say.

"Let's go back to the hotel," he whispered in between kisses.

She barely remembered Jarrid driving back to the hotel. The warmth of his arms, the tenderness of his kisses. That's all she was aware of. That's all she wanted to know.

As she entered the lobby, she heard soft piano music emanating from the restaurant lounge. A male voice sang words of romantic love and promises of remaining together for always.

When Jarrid kissed her hand and his eyes met hers, she knew he heard the love words and felt the intimacy of the moment, too.

Her legs felt trembly as she walked with him to her room. He unlocked the door and set her luggage inside.

She was very aware of the king-size bed, waiting for their naked bodies to make love.

She could see the yearning in Jarrid's eyes, the same aching she felt deep inside.

"If you need me," he said. "Just knock on the connecting door."

Then Jarrid left her room, keeping his promise not to put any pressure on her.

She stared at the door separating her body from his. All she had to do was knock, turn the knob and she would fall into his arms, on his bed, naked under the sheets.

She forced her mind away from her sensual thoughts and went out on the small balcony facing the Pacific Ocean. She noticed the half wooden wall between her balcony and his. She could see the light emanating from his room. She yearned to call out to him and invite him back to her.

Instead, she returned to her room, slipped off her clothes and stepped into the shower. Just as she turned on the faucet, she could hear Jarrid's shower turn on, too. She pictured him stark-naked as the water flowed down his vitally masculine frame.

She quickly finished her shower, reminding herself over and over that she was in Santa Barbara to help Jarrid's business and solidify Pam's relationship with him, nothing more.

After drying off, she searched her suitcase for her nightgown and realized that she'd been so nervous packing for the weekend trip that she'd only brought her cotton robe.

As she slipped the robe over her nude body, she felt the salty ocean air blowing in through the open balcony door. Wanting to feel safe during the night, she closed and locked the door and then turned the switch of the air conditioner for ventilation. But it wouldn't go on.

She felt the powerful impulse to knock on the connecting door and ask for Jarrid's help, but she knew it would just be an excuse to be with him. And she didn't dare, knowing how much she desired to make love to him.

She knocked into the air-conditioning unit several times with her fist, hoping it would turn on.

Just then, she heard a knock on the connecting door. She held her breath as the door slowly opened.

Jarrid stood there wearing green boxer shorts. His muscular chest was bronzed and bare. His curly hair was still damp from his shower.

"I heard banging," he said in a husky voice. "I was worried about you."

"The air conditioner won't go on."

"I'll take a look at it."

As he stood close to her at the unit, all she was conscious of was his hard muscular body close to hers.

He removed the cover from the thermostat. "Geez, look at all that dust," he said. "The thermostat won't register the temperature in the room." He blew out the dust, carefully put the cover back on and turned on the unit. A whirring sound echoed through the room.

Suddenly a gush of icy air blew on her. "It's icy cold!" she burst out.

She felt Jarrid's arms go around her. "Better?"

She nodded and pressed her face against his broad bare chest. She could hear his heart pumping faster. Her hands rested on his warm naked back.

"I need you, Becky," he whispered against her hair. "I need you so much."

"Jarrid, hold me tight," she whispered back. She lifted her face to his and met his lips with hers.

He crushed her body to his as he hungrily tasted her. She felt him loosen the tie of her robe. She sucked in her breath as his hands slid under the robe and cupped her aching breasts.

A zillion warning bells went off in her head. She knew

she should stop right then. But all she was aware of was her intense need for Jarrid. She wanted to give all of herself to him. Her heart, her soul and her body.

As he slid her robe down her bare shoulders, he openly gazed at her trembling nakedness.

"You're so sexy, so sexy," he said in a hoarse voice.

Jarrid trailed his finger along her neck and slid it between the crevice of her breasts, sending a waterfall of tingles trickling down her skin.

As he circled each nipple with his thumb, his gaze linked to hers, like he was looking deeply into her soul. With his eyes still on her, he slid his hand down her belly and reached the pulsating area between her legs. He caressed her pleasure zone until her eyes closed and she moaned with orgasmic pleasure.

"Becky, I want to make love to you," he whispered, as though he wanted to be sure she felt the same way, too.

Unable to restrain her love, she surrendered to the searing need for him that had been building since the moment she met him.

"I want you so much, Jarrid," she heard herself whisper back.

Jarrid slowly lowered her onto the bed. Then he slid off his boxers. Her heart pounded as his huge manhood stood erectly in front of her. The area between her thighs throbbed, aching to feel him inside of her.

As he lowered his muscular body on top of hers, his tongue dipped into her mouth, mingling and dancing with hers. Her breath came quickly as she felt his masculinity against her belly. Her skin burned with a passion she'd never experienced before.

All she wanted, all she desired, was to become one with Jarrid.

She reached down and caressed his hardness with her

fingers. He groaned and grew larger in her hand. He spread her legs and slipped his manhood deep inside her.

"Oh, Jarrid!" she called out, feeling an exquisite oneness with him that permeated her entire being.

As he moved in and out of her, he gazed deeply into her eyes. "Becky," he whispered. "I love you. I love you so much!"

Hot tears filled her eyes, and the words she'd yearned to say for so long flowed from her heart to her lips.

"Jarrid, I love you, too," she whispered back.

Ecstatic electricity rushed through her veins as Jarrid grew explosively large inside of her. He gripped her buttocks, pressing her tight against him. His muscles tensed and his body trembled on top of her.

"Becky, Becky," he lovingly moaned over and over.

Then he exploded deep inside of her. Fiery sensations coursed through her as she spasmed in response to his release. And in that moment, she felt her soul fuse with his.

Afterward, as she lay in the comfort of his arms, she felt a wave of peacefulness. He tenderly kissed her forehead, her eyes, her nose, her lips.

"I feel so close to you, Becky," he whispered. "So close."

Becky didn't remember falling asleep in Jarrid's arms. She felt him gently stroking her naked back, soothing her, comforting her with his warm love.

When the morning sun filtered through the balcony window, her eyes slowly opened. For a moment she couldn't remember where she was.

Then she saw Jarrid lying naked and asleep beside her in bed. His large palm lay tenderly over her naked breast. A feeling of dread overcame her when she realized what she'd done.

She slipped out of Jarrid's arms, trying not to wake him.

She went into the bathroom and closed the door. Her forehead ached. Her stomach felt ill.

What about her twin? How was she going to confess to her sister that she'd given her heart, her soul and now her body to Jarrid?

A burning guilt seared through her veins, not only because she'd gone over the boundary line with the man her sister loved. But also because after experiencing the ultimate intimacy with Jarrid, she wanted to go back in that room and make love to him all over again.

Nine

Jarrid's eyes slowly opened to the golden morning sunshine. "Becky," he whispered, reaching for her next to him, feeling an overwhelming love for her.

When he found her side of the bed empty, he noticed the bathroom door closed. He contentedly lay on the bed, knowing she was with him, feeling she would always be at his side.

He could still feel her heart pounding against his chest as he passionately joined his body with hers.

When he told her that he loved her, she said she loved him, too. That was the first time Becky had ever spoken the words.

Just then he heard the telephone ringing in his room. He pulled back the sheets, slipped on his boxer shorts and went to answer the phone.

When Becky heard the connecting door close, she left the bathroom and quickly threw on her robe. How was she going to face Jarrid when she felt so guilty about making love to him?

Yet, for her sister's sake, she had to act like everything was perfect, that she loved him, that their passionate evening together was all that she'd dreamed it would be.

And it was. Oh, how it was! Jarrid was her fantasy man come to life. He'd brought out the passionate, sensual, uninhibited womanly part of herself that she never knew existed. And he said that he loved her. He loved her.

She stared at the hotel telephone. She felt the powerful urge to call Pam. She needed to confess that she'd made a horrible mistake, praying that her sister would forgive her.

However, what tortured her the most was that she could never share with her twin her real feelings about Jarrid. She could never tell her sister that making love to Jarrid was the most ecstatic moment of her life. That secret had to remain locked in her heart forever.

In his room, Jarrid couldn't believe his ears. "Mr. Harrison," he said into the phone, "are you saying that I've got the job?"

"Absolutely, Jarrid," Mr. Harrison replied.

He was so stunned that he could barely hear Mr. Harrison apologize for canceling their appointment, explaining that he was still at his home in Beverly Hills because he had to make an emergency trip with his wife to Europe later that day.

"But Mr. Harrison," Jarrid added, still astounded, "I haven't shown you any of my designs for your house."

"Jarrid, I'm not worried at all," Mr. Harrison said. "Last night my wife convinced me not to delay hiring you. It seems that Becky has promoted you to many clients at the salon, and my wife is afraid that if we don't snatch you up, we'll have to wait in a long line for your services."

Jarrid glanced at the closed connecting door, wanting to thank Becky for her faith in him, needing to tell her that she already felt like a wife to him.

"Mr. Harrison, I promise I'll create an entertainment system that will fit your every need," he said with confidence.

"Jarrid, I'm hoping that you can drive back to Santa Barbara again next weekend with Becky, all expenses paid," Mr. Harrison continued. "I plan to make arrangements with a few audio and video manufacturers that I know to set up a private demonstration at my studio. We'll feature the newest home theater equipment that the public hasn't even seen yet. Then we can choose the innovative components you will install. I also plan to invite several of my business associates who might be interested in your services."

"That's terrific!" Jarrid burst out. "Next weekend works for me. I'll help you pick out the finest quality equipment on the market."

Jarrid heard a voice in the background of Mr. Harrison's phone. "My wife just reminded me," Mr. Harrison added. "She has been trying to get Becky all morning but has been unable to reach her. If you connect with her, can you ask if she could come over at noon to style my wife's hair before we leave?"

"I'll tell Becky right away," he replied. "If there's a problem, I'll have her call your wife back. Otherwise, she'll be there at noon."

Jarrid hung up the phone, still feeling lightheaded that he'd gotten the job. He quickly knocked on the connecting door. "Becky, can I come in?"

He couldn't wait to share the incredible news with the woman he loved *and* his partner in business.

"Sure, come in, Jarrid," he heard her say. He thought her voice sounded somewhat distant, but he was too excited to think twice about it.

When Jarrid walked in, Becky was already dressed. She was folding her robe into her suitcase. Her hair was still wet from a shower. Her lips were freshly colored in pink. He wasn't sure if she was avoiding his eyes or if he was just being paranoid.

"Becky, are you sorry about last night?" he couldn't help but ask.

She looked at him. "Jarrid, it was the most beautiful experience of my life."

He smiled and drew her into his arms. "Me, too," he whispered, touching her lips with his. "Mr. Harrison just called. He postponed my appointment with him this morning, *but* he hired me over the phone to design his home entertainment system!"

"He did? He really did?" Her eyes were glowing. "Without showing him a design? How could that be?"

A rush of love filled his chest. "You got it for me, Becky." He tenderly kissed her lips and quickly added that Mrs. Harrison needed her to hurry back to Los Angeles and do her hair before they left for Europe.

"Let's go!" Becky said excitely. "I don't want anything to mess up your opportunity to work with Mr. Harrison."

He held on to her a moment longer. "Mr. Harrison invited the two of us, all expenses paid, to return next weekend to attend a private demonstration he's arranging."

"Us?" she repeated, looking unsure.

"Well, yeah," he hesitantly replied. "I thought you'd want to go with me."

"Yes, sure, of course," she rushed on, anxiously glancing at her watch. "We better get back to L.A. so I won't be late for Mrs. Harrison."

During the drive back, Jarrid noticed Becky nervously biting her thumbnail and constantly glancing at her watch. She hadn't said two words to him since they left the hotel.

She seemed pressured, and he thought it had to do with making it back on time for her appointment.

Jarrid stared straight ahead as he drove along Pacific Coast Highway, feeling frustrated with himself. He still hadn't asked Becky to marry him like he'd planned. He knew he couldn't ask her now, not when her mind was so preoccupied.

He decided to wait. Then he would have a little more time to come up with the perfect plan to propose to her. A marriage proposal she wouldn't be able to refuse.

Back at her apartment, after styling Mrs. Harrison's hair, Becky sat on the bed with her hand on the phone, wrestling with how she was going to tell her sister that she'd made love to Jarrid.

Her fingers felt stiff as she dialed Pam's apartment in New York. When she got the answering machine, she could barely get the words out, asking Pam to call her right away from Japan.

She didn't know how much time had passed as she paced her apartment, thinking of a way to explain to her sister that she never meant to hurt her. She never meant to fall in love with Jarrid.

The ringing of the phone startled her. She yanked up the receiver, dreading the words she had to say.

"Beck, I just got your message," her sister said in a rushed voice across the intercontinental line. "I'm at a meeting in Tokyo, so I can't talk for long." She lowered her voice. "Brian, the new account executive, is right next to me."

Becky bit her bottom lip so hard that she could almost taste blood. "Pam, there's something I need to tell you."

"Beck, wait, Brian just left the room." Her twin's voice rose with excitement. "Beck, you won't believe this, but I'm in love with him!"

Becky wasn't sure she heard right. "In love with who?"

"Brian—the new account exec who's supposed to take my place," Pam hurried on. "I didn't want to tell you until I was absolutely sure. But he told me that he loves me, too. He and I are revving up so much advertising business for the company that we've been offered a promotion to become advertising partners. We'll be flying to L.A. four times a year to do business, so we can still be together sometimes, Beck!"

Becky's mind was spinning in every direction. "What about your job with Charlotte?"

"Don't worry. I already called her and explained the entire situation," her sister replied. "I recommended a friend of mine who's highly respected in the advertising business and is moving to Los Angeles. Charlotte's completely satisfied with the arrangement. So there's no problem, Beck."

"How can you say that, Pam?" The words stuck in her throat. "What about Jarrid? How can you hurt him all over again?"

"Beck, it's not like that at all," her sister hurried on. "Don't you see? My zany plan worked."

"What plan?"

"To get you and Jarrid together!"

"What are you talking about?"

"From the moment you met Jarrid at the gym, I knew you were falling in love with him," her twin said. "But I also knew you'd never believe that Jarrid could fall in love with you after what happened between you and Darryl. So I purposely asked you to play me so you'd open up completely to him. And it worked, didn't it?"

Becky sat down, feeling dizzy and confused. "Are you saying you were never in love with Jarrid?"

"That's right, Beck," Pam explained. "But I couldn't

tell you that because you wouldn't have gone along with my plan.''

"But Jarrid thinks I'm you!'' she blurted. "How am I going to tell him that I'm not who he thinks I am?''

"I'll handle it,'' her sister replied. "I'm leaving Japan tomorrow and plan to stop over in L.A. to see you. I'll talk to Jarrid in person. I'll explain the whole story to him. He's so in love with you, Beck. He won't care.''

Becky swallowed. "You're wrong, Pam.''

"Please, Beck, don't start doubting Jarrid's love for you,'' her sister pushed on. "Then my nutty plan will have failed.'' Her sister hurried on about how her boyfriend, Brian, would be with her when she stopped in Los Angeles and how she couldn't wait for Becky to meet him. "Beck, don't be mad at me. Because you helped me, too. After hearing all your love stories about being with Jarrid, I realized that *I* could fall permanently in love with one man, too, just like you. And now I have, Beck. I've got to go. I love you, sis!''

Becky felt caught in a tornado of emotion. She should've felt exhilarated that she was free to love Jarrid. But she didn't. Because no matter how much her sister wanted her plan to work, the fact was that Jarrid wasn't in love with *her*. He was in love with the memory of her twin.

Becky knew it would be wrong to let Pam tell Jarrid the truth. She had to tell him herself. And the moment she told him that she wasn't the outgoing, sensual woman he was in love with, she would lose him forever.

Monday morning at the jewelry store in Westwood, Jarrid stared at all the sparkling diamond engagement rings inside the glass display.

He'd made up his mind. No more doubting the love he shared with Becky. No more waiting for the right moment. The perfect time would never come. He had to ask her now.

The elderly saleswoman took out several rings for him to look at. "Would you like an oval, pear or round diamond ring?" she asked.

"Oval," Jarrid replied, gazing at the shimmering stone set in white gold, wanting this ring to be totally different from the ring he'd handed Becky on her prom night.

He was going to surprise her. He was going to propose to her and then slip the beautiful engagement ring on her finger, just like he had wanted to do seven years ago.

"Excellent choice," the saleswoman said, carefully placing the diamond ring into a black velvet box. "The woman you love is going to find your proposal irresistible."

He anxiously squeezed the velvet box in his hand. "I hope so."

"Young man," the woman began, looking at him with wise eyes. "You should radiate total confidence when you ask a lady to marry you. Then she will surely respond with a yes."

"You're right," he said, his tone lifting.

"Good luck in your new marriage."

"Thank you," he said, warmly. "Thanks so much."

At her apartment, Becky picked up the telephone for the thousandth time to call Jarrid and then put it back down. She had wanted to call him from the salon during her morning break, but she couldn't bring herself to do it with Sherry and the other hair stylists around. So she came home at lunchtime to try to make the call.

What would she say to him? That she's not Pam? That she could never be the type of woman he needed, the type of woman he thought he'd fallen in love with?

Filled with turmoil, she went into the kitchen, trying to get up the courage to call him. She looked for something to eat for lunch. But her refrigerator shelves were empty because she hadn't gone grocery shopping.

She sat down at the kitchen table with a sheet of paper and pencil. Maybe if she wrote down what she wanted to tell him first, she'd feel more comfortable speaking to him. She scribbled the words, "I'm not who you think I am. I'm not the woman you're in love with. I'm not—"

She crumpled the paper and hurled it into the trash can. The fact was she didn't want to tell him the truth. She wanted to still be Pam so he would continue loving her.

She forced herself to pick up the telephone. She would ask if she could meet him. She would say she had something very important to talk about. She had to do it face-to-face.

As she began dialing Jarrid's number, the ringing of her doorbell momentarily startled her. She quickly put down the phone and opened her front door.

"Beck, it's me!" her identical twin sister said with bright eyes and a big smile.

"Pam!" she cried out, closing her arms around her sister. "Oh, Pam, it's so good to see you!"

Standing beside Pam, looking a bit awkward, was a tall, thin, well-dressed man with straight black hair stylishly combed back and handsome, chiseled features.

"Beck, this is my fiancé, Brian," Pam said, proudly.

"Welcome to our family, Brian!" Becky said, giving him a hug, wanting him to know that he was completely accepted.

Brian frowned. "Now, how am I going to tell the two of you apart?"

Pam mischievously grinned. "Brian, you'll just have to see us naked because Becky doesn't have a heart tattoo like I have on my—"

"Pam!" Becky blurted, shocked as usual by her sister's boldness.

"Brian knows I'm a little crazy," Pam said, lightly kissing him on the lips.

Becky suddenly felt a deep sadness as she thought about Jarrid, realizing he didn't know her at all. He only thought of her as being Pam, his old girlfriend.

Her twin didn't miss it. "Don't worry about Jarrid," Pam said, slipping her arm through Becky's and leading her into the bedroom.

Becky saw Brian sit down on her sofa and start reading the newspaper to give the two of them a couple of private moments together.

As her sister changed into jeans and a blouse, Becky said, "Pam, I'm scared I'm going to lose Jarrid."

"You won't, silly," her sister said, reassuredly. "When I explain to him the entire situation, he's going to think I'm as tricky and crafty as ever. And then he's going to hold on to you, love you and never let you go."

"But he's not in love with me, Pam," she insisted. "He fell for you, and when he finds out that I'm not you—"

"It's going to all work out," her twin said, giving Becky a warm hug. Then Pam walked back to where Brian was waiting. "Brian and I are starved for lunch, Beck. I'm so tired of eating restaurant food. Can we fix sandwiches here?"

"My fridge is bare," Becky said, quickly grabbing her wallet. "I'll run to the grocery store and buy us some cold cuts, rolls and potato salad. You two cozy up while I'm gone."

Becky glanced back and saw Brian slip his arm around her sister's waist and pull her onto his lap. She watched her sister snuggle against her man, feeling the same contentment and excitement she'd felt in Jarrid's arms.

A deep anguish overwhelmed her, knowing the man she loved would disappear from her life when he found out she was a big phony.

Becky was so distressed that she hurried out of her apartment forgetting to close the door behind her. She hopped into her car and took off for the grocery store with her love for Jarrid pervading her every thought.

Jarrid tried to observe the speed limit on Venice Boulevard, but it was difficult because of how nervous he felt. He could no longer wait for the perfect moment to propose to Becky. He had to do it now. He called the salon, and Sherry said Becky went home for lunch.

He turned the corner and parked in front of her apartment building. He anxiously held the black velvet box in his hand. This time he wasn't going to hand her the box to open. He lifted the velvety lid and gingerly took out the shimmering diamond engagement ring, closing his palm protectively around the white gold.

In a few magical moments, he planned to slip the ring around her finger before she had a chance to say no.

He locked his van door and walked toward her apartment. That's when he noticed that her door was ajar. He hesitated for a second. He glanced at the oval diamond in his hand.

I can't live without her, he told himself. *I'm not going to let her get away this time.*

With a jolt of energy, Jarrid walked up to Becky's apartment. He was just about to knock on her open door when his hand stopped in midair.

He felt like a steel fist slammed into his gut when he saw Becky on the sofa, sitting on the lap of another man.

She was so engrossed in the guy that she didn't even know he was at the door.

Jarrid's heart twisted in his chest when he saw her hug and kiss the man. And then, in the midst of his horror, she whispered, audible enough for him to hear, "I love you. You're the only man for me!"

His throat went desert dry. He could barely breathe. He

clenched his fists so tight that he felt the diamond ring digging into the palm of his hand like a knife.

Unable to control the hurt and anger rising within him, Jarrid opened his palm and stared at the ring that no longer had any meaning to him. He glanced up at Becky blending comfortably with another man.

Blinded by fury and pain, he was just about to shove the ring into his pocket when his elbow banged against her apartment door. He didn't even remember if the ring made it into his pocket.

"Jarrid!" he heard Becky call out as he turned away from her door. Her voice sounded a little strange to him, probably because she felt so guilty and shocked that he had found her out.

He kept walking, unable to respond to her. His heart was shut tight. He felt hollow inside. He heard her call out his name a few more times, but he barreled into his van and sped off.

Becky parked and carried up a grocery bag containing whole wheat bread, cold cuts, Muenster cheese, lettuce, tomatoes and cole slaw.

Her few moments alone in the grocery store hadn't cleared her mind at all. She was still filled with anxiety about talking to Jarrid. Maybe she and Pam could tell him together. Then he'd see why she had pretended to be Pam. Maybe he would understand. Maybe he would forgive her. Maybe, maybe, maybe!

As she hurried toward her apartment, she noticed that her apartment door was open. She realized she'd forgotten to close it when she left.

The moment she stepped inside, she saw the disturbed look on her sister's face. A feeling of alarm suddenly hit her.

"Pam, what's wrong?" she asked, noticing her twin glance worriedly at Brian.

"Jarrid was just here."

"Jarrid?" she repeated under her breath, feeling like something awful had just happened but not knowing what.

"Beck, he saw Brian and me kissing," her sister said, distraught. "He thought I was you."

"Oh, no!" The bag of groceries slipped out of her hand, and the food spewed onto the floor.

Without thinking, she ran to her apartment door and glanced out, desperately wanting to catch him, needing to tell him it was all a horrible, horrible mistake.

At the doorway she could hear Pam talking to her from the living room, but the words didn't register in her brain. As she turned to her sister, her eye caught something twinkle on the ground.

She bent down and saw a sparkling oval diamond engagement ring lying near her doorway. Her heart wrenched as she gently picked it up and held it in her hand.

Her mind was reeling. Hurricane emotions rushed through her. Jarrid had come by to propose marriage to her. He was going to give her the beautiful diamond engagement ring to bond his love with her forever.

She swallowed, remembering Pam's diary, remembering how he'd given her sister an engagement ring on her prom night and how Pam had turned him down.

She momentarily forgot her own grief, her own turmoil. All she could think about was how devastated Jarrid must be after being torturously rejected twice.

"Beck, it's all my fault," Pam said, touching her shoulder. "I've ruined everything."

"Pam, no, please—"

"We'll go to Jarrid's apartment right now," her twin said. "He'll see it was all a mistake."

Becky showed Pam the diamond ring in her hand. "He came over to ask *you* to marry him."

Pam stared at her. "No, he didn't, Beck. He was going to ask *you* to marry him."

Becky couldn't believe that, no matter how much she wanted to. "I need to talk to him. I want to tell him everything."

She had to give the engagement ring back to Jarrid. Because it was never for her, but always for Pam.

The moment her sister and Brian left the apartment for a while as she'd requested, Becky mustered up the courage and dialed Jarrid's store, but Pete said Jarrid wasn't there. Then she called his home phone number. She stared at the glittering oval diamond in her hand.

She wished she could wash away his pain. She wished she could tell him it was all a sorry joke. That she loved him. That she could never be in any man's arms but his.

But Jarrid's phone rang and rang. No answering machine picked up her call. She knew he didn't want to talk to her. She knew she was the last person in the cosmos that he ever wanted to see again.

Ten

———

In his brother's backyard, Jarrid angrily hurled the basketball toward the hoop. The ball banged against the metal rim and flew to the ground.

"Jarrid, what're you doing here on a week night?" Kenny asked with concern, retrieving the ball and throwing it back to him.

"I need some company," Jarrid managed to say, feeling a void inside that was bigger than outer space.

He couldn't go back to his lonely apartment. Not after seeing Becky in the arms of another man. He needed to be around his family. He needed to feel connected, because he suddenly felt more lost than he'd ever felt in his entire life.

Kenny studied him. "Did Becky break up with you?"

Jarrid deliberately threw the ball hard against the backboard. His eyes started to burn, but he turned away, not wanting his brother to see how scalded he felt inside.

"It's over," Jarrid said. "We're finished for good."

"Uncle Jarrid, who's finished?" Lizzy asked, running over and getting the basketball for him.

"Lizzy—" his brother began, obviously not wanting her to upset Jarrid even more.

"It's okay, Kenny," Jarrid cut in. "She needs to know, too." He squatted down to be eye-to-eye with her. "Becky and I aren't going together anymore."

"How come, Uncle Jarrid?" she asked. "I thought you were going to ask her to marry you."

Jarrid felt like his insides were being crushed by a vise. "It didn't work out, Lizzy."

Her innocent eyes filled with confusion. "Becky said no to you?"

He painfully flashed on Becky kissing that other guy. "Sort of."

"Can't you ask her again?" Lizzy suggested. "Maybe she was just in a bad mood. Maybe she'll say yes this time."

Kenny walked over and put his arm around his daughter's shoulders. "Lizzy, go ask Mommy when dinner's going to be ready."

"But I need to find out about Becky."

"Get going," his brother insisted.

Lizzy made a face. "Okaaaay."

Jarrid watched Lizzy run off, but he knew it wasn't finished with her. He knew how close his niece felt to Becky. And he knew how much Lizzy wanted Becky to be her aunt. He wanted that, too. And he truly believed that Becky felt the same way. How wrong he'd been.

"Jarrid, what the hell happened?" Kenny asked, throwing him the basketball.

"Becky's seeing another guy," he choked out. "I went to her apartment to propose. I had the engagement ring and everything. And there she was...with him."

"The Becky we met?" his brother asked, incredulously.

"But she doesn't seem like the type. She was so sweet, so loyal."

Jarrid slumped down into a patio chair. "It was her, Kenny. I got so teed off that I lost the damn ring."

"Geez." His brother sat in a chair across from him. "What did she say to you? She must've had an explanation."

"I didn't hang around to find out," he replied. "I just wanted out of there."

Just then Marie walked into the backyard with a worried look on her face. "Jarrid, are you okay? Lizzy told me that you and Becky broke up."

He swallowed. "I'm an available man again."

"I can't believe it," Marie said, shaking her head. "Becky seemed so sincere when she talked to me."

Jarrid stood up. He couldn't handle the wrenching pain of discussing Becky. "I've got to catch up on some work at the store."

He barely remembered leaving his brother's house. He felt in a fog as he drove, as though nothing was real to him anymore.

Not even the appointment he had in Santa Barbara next Saturday. He'd wanted Becky with him.

That night, as he sat at his desk in the cramped office at the back of his store, he thought of Becky being in his arms. He had offered his heart and soul for her to take. He had believed her when she said she loved him in the hotel room in Santa Barbara.

He forced himself to pull out the sample design he'd started to draw for the Harrisons' Santa Barbara house. From an imagined idea of what their home looked like, he began sketching built-in surround sound speakers in the living room, family room and bedrooms, but he abruptly stopped drawing.

Without Becky, expanding his store suddenly had no

meaning. The exhilarated feeling was gone. Without her sharing his life, he felt only half there.

In the darkness of the evening, Becky's heart pounded as she walked up to Jarrid's apartment door. She had tried a zillion times calling him at his store and at home, but his phone was never picked up. She even drove by his store, but the shades were down, and the lights were off.

She forced herself to knock, holding the engagement ring in her hand, trying to find the right words to ask for his forgiveness. She stood there for a few torturous minutes, but he didn't answer the door.

As Becky walked away, she was determined to keep calling Jarrid until he finally talked to her. She knew he was raw with emotion. She recognized he didn't trust her. What agonized her more than anything was knowing she would never hurt him by being with another man, not ever.

In her car she stared at the ring. For one instant she dared to slip it on her ring finger. Her heart pounded like a tom-tom in her chest thinking about being engaged to him.

Jarrid, oh, Jarrid, I love you so much, she silently whispered. Then she quickly took off the ring and put it into her bag beside Lizzy's quartz crystal.

She knew her love words would never be heard by Jarrid, not after he found out she lied, not after he learned she wasn't the woman of his dreams.

Late Saturday afternoon, at the private demonstration in Santa Barbara, Jarrid tried to concentrate on the entertainment components on display. Guests of Mr. Harrison were arriving. Their names were checked off on the invitation list at the front door.

Jarrid noticed his host talking to a couple of business associates. Mr. Harrison glanced over and smiled, letting Jarrid know that he was praising his talent to his friends after showing them Jarrid's designs for his Santa Barbara house.

Jarrid should have felt elated at Mr. Harrison's positive endorsement of his work. His business could soar to heights he'd never imagined. Instead, his eyes felt blurry from lack of sleep. His brain felt muddled from his chaotic thoughts.

Because Becky wasn't with him. Her name was still on the invitation list at the front door, but she wasn't at his side.

As Jarrid checked the display of high-tech modular speakers, he flashed on last night, right before he left for Santa Barbara. He was late and hurrying to lock his apartment door to leave, when his answering machine came on. It was Becky again. She said she needed to talk to him.

She'd called him several times, but he couldn't bring himself to pick up the phone. Because even though she had betrayed him, he realized that he hadn't stopped loving her.

That's what frustrated and angered him the most. The moment he heard her voice, he wanted to see her. He wanted to hold her. And he blamed himself that she had turned to another man.

How many times had he warned himself not to push her into the relationship before she was ready? He knew from his past experience with her that she needed a man who didn't pressure her, who didn't feel such an overwhelming need to be with her all the time.

"Jarrid, I want you to meet Frank Whittier and Paul Fielding," Mr. Harrison said, startling Jarrid out of his thoughts. "Both of these gentlemen are interested in hearing your ideas on designing private screening rooms in their homes."

"Tell me the size of the space," Jarrid replied, "and I'll draw up a sketch for each of you right now."

A rush of enthusiastic energy hit him. He instinctively glanced at the crowd entering the studio, needing to see

Becky, wanting to share the incredible business possibilities about to take place because of her. However, he realized he was searching for a love that was no longer in his life.

His mind flashed on the engagement ring. Losing the diamond was an omen to him.

It's over, he told himself. *She's out of your life for good.* He should never have fallen in love with her a second time, when she'd never loved him from the beginning.

He forced his attention back to Mr. Harrison and the businessmen.

Becky furiously drove up the Pacific Coast Highway toward Santa Barbara. Since she hadn't been able to get Jarrid on the phone, she'd stopped by his store. Pete told her that Jarrid had left early for Mr. Harrison's private demonstration. From the way Pete avoided her eyes, she could tell that Jarrid was still hurting bad.

Becky didn't waste a second. She had to talk to Jarrid right away. She had to tell him the truth. She knew how important this deal was to him. She wanted his mind to be free of the painful rejection he'd experienced at her apartment.

As she pressed her foot harder on the gas pedal, she hoped to catch a few moments alone with him at Mr. Harrison's studio. She hoped he would listen to her. Maybe he would be able to forget what he saw and go on with his life. She tried not to think about the fact that she would never be a part of his daily existence again.

She glanced at her bag on the car seat beside her. She'd brought the photograph of her and Pam so he would see the truth for himself. She also had the engagement ring to give back to him. The love ring he'd meant to put on her twin's finger, not hers.

As she drove, she touched the quartz crystal in her bag,

praying that the stone would give her the luck she desperately needed to get Jarrid to forgive her for tricking him.

She stared at the traffic ahead, feeling a crushing sensation in her chest, knowing the lucky crystal could never give her what she really wanted—the love of Jarrid—because it was never hers from the beginning.

Becky pulled into the parking lot and hurried to the front door, nervous about facing Jarrid, hoping he'd let her talk to him. As she entered the large studio, she saw that it was jammed with people viewing displays of imaging systems, digital processors and theater bass speakers. She sifted through the crowd trying to spot Jarrid. Her heartbeat quickened when she saw him.

He was at the far end of the studio pointing to sound equipment and simultaneously showing a drawing to Mr. Harrison and a couple of businessmen.

Her heart glowed with pride as Mr. Harrison smiled with satisfaction at Jarrid while the other men nodded with approval. She was sure that he was a big hit with them. She knew his dream of expanding his business would finally come true.

But her smile faded when she saw the sadness in Jarrid's eyes. He wasn't experiencing the happiness she knew he would be feeling if his heart hadn't been ripped in two. She had to get him alone. She had to make him see—

"Becky?" she heard someone say from behind her. She turned to see Mrs. Harrison, who added, "Isn't this an incredible crowd? My husband invited many of his business friends and clients. In fact, I believe that Jarrid is discussing entertainment systems with my husband right now."

Becky turned in Jarrid's direction, but many more guests had arrived, blocking her view. Mrs. Harrison started talking about the new hairstyle she'd seen in a magazine that she wanted to have done at her next salon appointment, and she guided Becky to a corner of the studio to chat.

As Jarrid explained to Mr. Harrison and his associates how he would surround their private screening rooms with eight digital sound speakers, he caught sight of the back of a woman at the far end of the room. His heart hammered. The woman looked just like Becky.

Just then several guests moved in front of him, and he could no longer see her. As he moved to the side to get a better view, he spotted a couple embracing in the studio. His heart sank in his chest as he remembered Becky in the arms of another man.

He still couldn't believe that she had turned on him. Not after she had loved him so completely in the hotel room. Yet, why did he doubt that she could suddenly change her feelings about him when she'd done it seven years ago?

Just then Mr. Harrison shook Jarrid's hand. "Jarrid, I think you just made two more sales."

"Thank you so much, Mr. Harrison," he said, firmly shaking his hand and then the hands of the two business-men.

Feeling a sweet-and-sour elation, Jarrid impulsively searched the faces in the crowd for the woman that looked like Becky. Even though he knew he was imagining she was there, he still felt the urge to share his accomplishment with her.

He needed to hold her. He needed to tell her that she was the one who'd moved his life and his business forward. She had skyrocketed his entire existence.

That's what murdered him the most inside. He was still dreaming about his love for her. He couldn't let go of her. He wanted to go on believing that he still shared a deep love with her, a love that nothing could destroy.

Becky stood in the shadows of the guests with Mrs. Harrison still chatting. From far away, she thought she saw

Jarrid glance in her direction. His eyes radiated a charged excitement and also a deep loneliness at the same time.

At that moment she knew he'd gotten more work from Mr. Harrison's associates. She felt the urge to rush into his arms. She wanted to tell him how joyful she felt that his business goals were coming to fruition. She yearned to share in the thrill of his very special day.

Just then Becky saw Jarrid leaving the studio with Mr. Harrison and the two businessmen. As she excused herself from Mrs. Harrison, she moved through the crowd, wishing she could go with him. From the front window, she saw him get into Mr. Harrison's shiny black limousine.

For an instant he glanced back at the studio, almost as though he knew she was there. Then the limousine door closed, and the car drove off.

Standing alone, Becky realized that her moments of ecstatic love with Jarrid were just a fantasy. She was never a real part of his life. She lived in the shadow of her sister. The joyful closeness, being snugly wrapped in his arms, being told he loved her, none of it had ever belonged to her.

She knew she would have to wait until Jarrid returned to Los Angeles before she could talk to him, so she left the studio.

As she drove her car, she saw the neon sign of the Blue Sea Hotel up ahead on the road. Her heart lurched thinking about the evening Jarrid had made love to her.

Her foot eased up on the gas pedal as she slowed down her car. The beautiful memories of her intimate night with him flashed through her mind. She wanted one last moment to linger on the closeness and sensual feelings she'd shared with him, because she would never have them again.

Without a second thought she turned off at the next exit and pulled her car into the hotel parking lot. She got out and walked onto the beach to the shoreline under the starlit sky. She glanced up at the balcony of the room where she and Jarrid had become one. The balcony doors were open, and she could see a couple laughing and toasting glasses of wine. Then their lips met.

She turned away and stared at the darkness of the Pacific Ocean. Foamy white water of the waves drifted up to the shoreline near her shoes. She couldn't wash away the love surging through her heart. She would always love Jarrid, no matter how many years drifted between them, no matter how far away he was from her.

The evening air felt chilly, and she wrapped her arms around her chest. She knew she should forget her love night with him, but she needed to hold the vision close to her for just a few more precious moments.

In the back seat of Mr. Harrison's limousine, Jarrid couldn't concentrate on the businessmen discussing their stock options and ways to increase their company revenues.

He stared out the tinted windows at the evening shadows of the Spanish architecture of Santa Barbara, wishing Becky was in the seat next to him.

When he'd left Mr. Harrison's studio, he thought he'd seen her at the window watching him. He knew his mind was acting crazy. She was so steady in his thoughts that he was seeing her everywhere.

"Jarrid, I hope you don't mind," Mr. Harrison began, "but we would like to take you to a late dinner at the Santa Barbara Country Club."

"Sounds great," Jarrid replied, appreciating Mr. Harrison's gesture. "But could I first make a stop at my room at the Blue Sea Hotel to pick up my dinner jacket?"

"No problem," he replied, leaning forward to tell his driver.

Jarrid left the limousine waiting in front of the hotel. As he headed toward his room, he abruptly stopped walking.

He thought he saw the silhouette of Becky standing under the moonlight in the sand facing the Pacific Ocean. He squinted his eyes, sure he was mistaking someone else for her, just like he'd done at the studio.

But as he walked closer, his heart pumped wildly in his chest. Her strawberry blond hair blew softly in the ocean wind. Her calf-length dress clung to her shapely legs, and the scent of full-bloomed roses filled the sea air.

For a moment he forgot about the aching pain in his heart. He forgot that she betrayed him.

"Becky," he whispered as he neared her.

When she whirled around and saw him, her cheeks immediately flushed. Her emerald eyes softened as she looked at him.

For that instant Jarrid felt the same overwhelming love for her. Then the searing vision of her in the arms of another man pounded at his skull.

"Becky, what are you doing here?" he demanded.

Becky wanted to put her arms around Jarrid. She yearned to whisper how much she loved him, but she saw the pain in his eyes, the pain she'd caused.

"I went to Mr. Harrison's studio to see you," she replied in an unsteady voice. "But you were so busy. Jarrid, I want to tell you what happened when you came to my apartment."

His jaw tensed. "You don't have to explain. You made it very clear where you stand with me."

"No, Jarrid."

"I saw you, Becky." His voice cracked as he looked off toward the darkness of the Pacific Ocean. "I don't need a road map for details."

"It wasn't me you saw."

"Becky, come on."

"My identical twin sister was at my apartment when you arrived."

"Really?" he shot back in a mocking tone. "And I'm my brother's identical triplet."

"Jarrid—" she choked out, desperately wanting to put his shattered heart back together again. "Please let me prove it to you. I have something to show you in my car."

Before he could protest, she hurried toward her car, hoping the torture in his eyes would disappear once he saw the truth, praying he would forgive her.

The muscles of Jarrid's body felt tight as he followed Becky. He could hear laughter and piano music emanating from the restaurant bar. He could see the black limousine waiting for him at the curb.

He knew he should tell her to forget whatever game she was trying to play with him. Because he wasn't going to be the sucker anymore. Yet, he couldn't stop himself from giving her a chance. He couldn't curtail the powerful feelings he still had for her.

"Jarrid, look at this picture," Becky begged, handing him a photograph. "This is me, Jarrid, and *this* is my sister, Pam."

Jarrid stared in disbelief at the color photograph. There was Becky with her arm around Becky. "I don't understand. Is this another one of your jokes?"

"Jarrid, you knew my sister when she was in high school," she explained. "Her name was Becky, just like mine." She rushed on about how she and her twin were separated at birth and never knew the other existed. She told him about how her sister had found her and then changed her same first name, Becky, to their birth mother's first name, Pam.

Jarrid's mind felt chaotic as he looked from Becky to the photograph and then back to Becky.

"You're Becky's identical twin?" he asked in disbelief. "Why didn't you tell me the first day we met?"

"I did!" Becky replied. "You wouldn't believe me."

"Is that why you didn't remember our mutual friend Connie?" he asked, feeling a stream of clarifying relief. "And why you hated raw fish?"

When she nodded, his heart filled with hope.

"When you came to my apartment," she added, "I was at the supermarket, and my sister was there with her new boyfriend, Brian."

"The supermarket!"

He wanted to howl with elation that the horror of what he'd seen at her apartment was an illusion. Becky had been true to him. He could feel his love for her suddenly surging through his heart again.

"Jarrid, I'm sorry I pretended to be my sister," Becky hurried on. "But she begged me to. She asked me to get close to you until she moved to Los Angeles. She wanted me to get you to forgive her for hurting you in high school. I never felt comfortable playing her, but she's my sister. I had to do it."

His muscles tightened. "Then the whole time," he began with difficulty, "you were only with me for your sister?"

"Yes," she replied in a low voice.

He felt like the air had been sucked out of his lungs.

As she reached into her bag, he thought he saw something fall out of her bag, but his attention was riveted to the oval diamond engagement ring she pulled out.

"I guess you accidentally dropped this ring before you had a chance to give it to my sister."

As she put the love diamond into his palm, her warm fingers touched his hand. He felt the impulse to close his hand over hers, but she slid her fingers away and quickly clasped her hands together.

His throat constricted. "Thanks for bringing me the ring."

"I'm really sorry for whatever I put you through," she rushed on. "I never meant to cause you any trouble."

His heart burned like a fiery coal in his chest. "It's okay," he said. His dream of being with Becky shattered into tiny pieces right before his eyes. "I appreciate your telling me the truth."

Just then he saw the window of the black limousine roll down. Mr. Harrison glanced out in his direction.

Becky noticed, too. "You better not keep your new customers waiting."

"Yeah, right."

Before he could say another word to her, she hurried to her car. He felt the urge to go after her. He wanted to find out who she really was, versus the imagined person he thought her to be. But she drove out of the Blue Sea Hotel parking lot without looking back.

Feeling crushed, Jarrid was about to head for the limousine when he noticed something shimmering on the ground. He picked up a small crystal. He realized the stone had fallen from Becky's bag when she was pulling out the engagement ring.

He quickly looked in her direction. But her car had merged with the red taillights of the boulevard traffic, out of his life forever.

As Becky drove back to Los Angeles, she fought the tears blurring her eyes. She barely saw the white wash of the surfing waves of Zuma Beach in the darkness, rushing past her car. She didn't notice the modernistic ocean-front Malibu houses lining Pacific Coast Highway.

All she felt was the tearing apart of her heart, leaving Jarrid at the Blue Sea Hotel.

As she drove, Becky reached into her bag for Lizzy's quartz crystal, needing to hold on to the only link she had left to him.

When she didn't feel the stone against her fingers, she quickly pulled her car off to the shoulder of Pacific Coast Highway near Will Rogers State Beach.

She frantically dumped everything out of her bag onto the seat. Her lipstick, wallet, comb, tissue pack and checkbook fell out. But her lucky stone was gone.

Feeling like she was suffocating, Becky opened her car window and breathed in the ocean air. She stared at the expanse of empty evening beach. The half-moon glittered off the sand and sea. The lifeguard stand was barren, just like her heart.

Why was she torturing herself? She knew all along that Jarrid was in love with her sister. He had never loved *her*. Why was she pining over a love she never had?

The cool salty night air filtered into the car chilling her skin. As she buttoned her dress to the neckline, she knew why she ached with a hollowness in her heart.

Because Jarrid had whirled her life around. She couldn't go back to the way she used to live, without him, knowing his apartment was so near, his store was a short distance away, and she would never be a part of his life again.

She started up the engine, realizing she had to make a drastic change in her life.

Early Sunday morning at his apartment, Jarrid abruptly woke up from a dream. His heart was racing. His skin felt moist with perspiration. He had been with Becky. She was lying in his arms, whispering that she loved him, that she would always be with him. And in the next moment she was gone.

Just then the phone rang. For an instant he thought it was Becky.

"Jarrid, where are you?" his sister-in-law's voice said over the line. "Lizzy's soccer game will be starting in fifteen minutes."

"I'll be right there," he quickly said, hanging up the phone, realizing he was so filled with turmoil about losing Becky that he'd forgotten he promised his niece he would be at her game.

He hopped out of bed, took a quick shower, and forced down a toasted English muffin. He spotted Becky's quartz crystal lying on his kitchen table.

He wanted to get it back to her. But how could he? She didn't want to see him. Her mission for her sister was over. She'd done her job. She wanted no part of him now.

Jarrid slipped the crystal into his jeans pocket and drove to Santa Monica Park. Lizzy's soccer game had already started. He hurried over to where Kenny and Marie were sitting on a blanket watching the game.

As he cheered for Lizzy, he took the quartz crystal out of his pocket and kept it in his hand. Even though he knew he shouldn't, he was still holding on to Becky in his mind.

Just then Lizzy was called out of the soccer game by her coach to rest, while another teammate got a chance to play. She ran to the blanket out of breath.

"Hi, Uncle Jarrid!" Lizzy said, hugging him.

As he hugged her back, the stone fell onto the blanket.

Lizzy quickly picked it up. "The crystal I gave Becky!"

"*You* gave it to her?" he asked, surprised.

"Why do you have it, Uncle Jarrid?"

"Becky accidentally dropped it."

"You need to get it back to her for me right away," his niece said with an urgency.

"Why?"

"Because without the crystal, Becky's dream won't ever come true."

"What dream, Lizzy?"

Just then her coach blew his whistle calling her back to the field. As his niece hurried to her teammates, Jarrid felt a jolt of energy. Lizzy and the crystal were his excuse to see Becky one last time. He slipped the stone into his pocket, hoping it might give him some luck, too.

Sunday night, Becky anxiously helped pack her twin sister's suitcases for her and Brian's return to New York. She could hear Brian in the living room on the telephone.

Pam looked at her, worried. "Beck, are you *sure* you want to move to New York? And so soon? What about Jarrid?"

Becky stopped packing her sister's clothes. "I can't stay in Los Angeles knowing I could bump into him at the gym or see him on the street."

Pam slumped onto the bed. "Beck, why don't you just tell Jarrid that you love him?"

"No, I can't do that."

"Listen to me, will you?" her sister pushed. "If I were you, I'd rush over to his place and tell him that I can't live without him."

"But I'm not *you,* Pam!" Her voice cracked. "Don't you see? You're the woman he fell in love with, not me."

There was a knock on the bedroom door, and Brian stuck his head into the room. "Pam, the cab to the airport is here."

"Brian, I'll be right there," her sister quickly said and then turned to her. "Beck, I'll call Jarrid. I'll tell him that you love him but you're shy and—"

"Please don't," she begged. "I can't hide behind you anymore. I don't want Jarrid coming to me because you talked him into it." Becky heard the horn of the taxi. "You better go with Brian."

Her twin held her tight. "I'll see you in New York. And don't worry about getting a job. You can stay at my apartment with me."

"I love you, sis," Becky whispered.

The moment her twin left, Becky knew she had to make

her moving plans fast, before she changed her mind. She picked up the phone. She had to call Sherry to tell her the truth about what happened between Jarrid, herself and Pam, and that she was moving to New York. Then she needed to call the owner of the salon and also all of her loyal clients to refer them to Sherry to do their hair.

On Monday, right before lunchtime, Jarrid parked his van in front of the Nouveau Hair Salon. He remembered Becky telling him that even though most salons were closed on Mondays, her shop was open and had plenty of customers.

He got out of his vehicle with Lizzy's quartz crystal securely in his pocket. He needed to look into Becky's eyes. He needed to find out how she'd really felt the moment he'd first kissed her. He needed to know if she had felt the same overpowering love he had felt on that evening when he'd made love to her.

And if Becky told him that she didn't love him, that she never felt an inkling of emotion for him, because she'd done it all for her sister, then he had to hear it for himself to settle the turmoil in his soul.

As Jarrid hurried into the salon, his gaze went straight to Becky's work station where a woman was seated in the swivel chair having her hair cut.

His heartbeat came to a staggering halt when he saw that the stylist trimming the customer's hair wasn't Becky. There was another hair cutter in her place.

Confused and not knowing what to do, he spotted Sherry, blow-drying a customer's hair. He quickly went over to her.

"Sherry," he began. "Where's Becky?"

He noticed Sherry hesitate. "Becky's not coming in today."

"She's not? Why? Have you spoken to her?"

"Jarrid," Sherry began, as though she were struggling to get the words out. "Becky has permanently left the job."

"You mean she quit?" he asked incredulously.

"She's moving to New York to live with her sister."

Jarrid felt like a lead pipe slammed into his chest. "To New York?"

His mind was reeling. He realized that Becky's need to be far away from him only confirmed that she never loved him. That she only pretended to care about him for her sister.

"Jarrid, I'm sorry," Sherry began. "Becky told me everything that happened. I just don't understand why she has to rush to move to New York."

"Because Becky wants nothing to do with me," he said.

"Are you sure about that, Jarrid?" Sherry asked.

He stared at her. "What do you mean?"

Her voice softened. "Maybe Becky's running away from her own feelings about you."

Jarrid couldn't believe what he was hearing. "Is that what she told you?" Could Becky really and truly love him?

"I can't say any more," she responded. "I'm having lunch with Becky for the last time today. I'll try to find out for you." Then she turned back to spray her client's hair.

"Sherry, can I talk to you after you finish with your customer?" he asked urgently, needing to find out as much as he could about Becky's leaving.

"I'll just be a few minutes," Sherry told him.

Jarrid anxiously sat in the waiting area, picking up hairstyle magazines and then putting them down. He had to figure out a way to talk to Becky. He had to find out the truth about her real feelings for him.

At a café in Beverly Hills, Becky glanced at her watch, waiting for Sherry to arrive for lunch. She had given notice at her apartment building, and her apartment lease was already grabbed up by a new tenant. Her belongings were all packed into boxes waiting to be shipped.

Yet she felt torn about moving to New York. She loved her job at the salon. And she loved Jarrid. Every time she thought about never seeing him again, her soul echoed with a loneliness she'd never experienced before. Because without Jarrid, only half of her felt alive.

But why torment herself? She couldn't live in Los Angeles knowing she would never be with him.

She glanced at her watch. Sherry was fifteen minutes late. She wondered if she should call the salon to see what was wrong but decided to wait a few more minutes.

She unconsciously reached for Lizzy's quartz crystal in her bag and realized again that she had lost it. Becky missed the stone so much. Now she had nothing at all from her precious moments sharing Jarrid's life.

She anxiously glanced at her watch again. Maybe something had happened. She went to the pay telephone in the restaurant.

Jarrid quickly parked his van in front of the café. He had asked Sherry to let him take her place at lunch with Becky. She had resisted, because she felt that Becky should be warned. But when he showed her the quartz crystal and told her he needed to talk to Becky more than anything, Sherry had gone along with his plan.

As Jarrid hurried into the restaurant, he saw Becky slipping coins into the pay telephone. An overwhelming love for her flowed through every vein in his body.

He forced himself not to get his hopes up. Because even though Sherry hinted that Becky cared for him, he couldn't be sure that she was as crazy in love with him as he was with her.

He walked over and gently touched her shoulder. "Becky," he whispered.

At the pay phone, just as Becky started talking to Sherry, she felt Jarrid's familiar touch on her shoulder and heard his deep voice calling her name.

She held her breath as she whirled around. "Jarrid, what are you doing here?"

"Can I talk to you, Becky?"

Talk to her? She wanted to melt into his arms. "Sure, I'll be off the phone in a sec."

He nodded and nervously stuck his hands into his pockets as he stepped a distance away to give her privacy.

When she returned to the phone, she heard Sherry say, "Jarrid insisted on seeing you. I couldn't say no to him. And then your sister called. I told her that Jarrid was having lunch with you. She was thrilled and said to tell you good luck!" And then Sherry hung up.

As Becky walked over to Jarrid, her heart pounded out of control being near him again. She wanted to feel his arms around her. She wanted to kiss him. She wanted to share every intimacy with him that she knew could never be hers.

Jarrid pulled out a chair for her at a table. As she sat down, her shoulder brushed against his hard chest, and that familiar electric current coursed through her body.

"I had to see you, Becky." He opened his large palm, and there was Lizzy's quartz crystal. "I knew you'd want this back."

"You found my lucky stone!" she said excitedly.

As he placed the crystal in her palm, she felt a surge of heat from his hand to hers.

"Lizzy misses you, Becky," he said.

"I miss her, too," she said, wanting to tell him how she deeply missed *him*, but didn't dare.

Instead, she added, "I wish I had never tricked you, Jarrid. If I could do it over again, I'd never take my sister's place with you. I'm really sorry."

"I'm not sorry, Becky," he said.

"You're not?" She squeezed the crystal in her hand.

"I feel very lucky I met you," he added. "Getting to know you has changed my life."

"It has?" she asked, in disbelief.

"More than any person I've ever known," he replied. "In fact, the reason I asked Sherry if I could take her place at lunch was because I was hoping we could start brand-new together."

She couldn't believe what she was hearing. "You mean, like we just met right now?"

He leaned closer to her at the table. "Can we pretend this lunch is our very first date?"

Could she? Oh, it felt like a dream! "Are you sure, Jarrid?" she asked in a shaky voice. "Because I'm not my sister anymore. I'm not like her at all. In fact, I'm just the opposite."

He gently touched her cheek. "Becky, I love *you*, not your sister."

"But you thought I was her. That's why—"

"Even when you were pretending to be her," he said, "your qualities, your personality, your beautiful giving feelings and sensual ways were what captivated me."

Sensual? Beautiful? Giving? Could he really be talking about her?

Before Becky could utter another syllable, Jarrid pulled something out of his pocket. He gently took her hand and slipped the sparkling oval engagement ring onto her finger.

"Becky, in my heart, this ring was always meant for you."

"For me?" She couldn't believe he wanted to be with

her, Becky Lawson, for always. "Are you sure, Jarrid? Are you really sure?"

"Becky, I love you," he said. "Everything about you is perfect for me."

Her eyes filled with tears. "Oh, Jarrid, I feel the same way about you!"

In the next moment, Becky was in his arms in the middle of the restaurant, holding him tight, never wanting to let him go.

With his lips against her hair, she heard Jarrid whisper, "Will you marry me, Becky?"

Becky was so choked up with emotion that she could hardly speak, but she heard herself whisper back, "I'll always be yours, Jarrid, always!"

As Becky's lips met Jarrid's for a sensual kiss of love, she squeezed the lucky crystal in her hand, knowing Lizzy's magic had really worked!

She couldn't wait to call her twin. She had to tell Pam that she would be in New York soon, but she would be visiting with Jarrid, the love of her life.

Because Becky had found her soul mate—Jarrid Browning—the man who was destined to be with her forever!

* * * * *

Return to the Towers!

In March
New York Times bestselling author

NORA ROBERTS

brings us to the Calhouns' fabulous
Maine coast mansion and reveals the
tragic secrets hidden there for generations.

For all his degrees, Professor Max Quartermain has a
lot to learn about love—and luscious Lilah Calhoun is
just the woman to teach him. Ex-cop Holt Bradford is
as prickly as a thornbush—until Suzanna Calhoun's
special touch makes love blossom in his heart.
And all of them are caught in the race to solve
the generations-old mystery of a priceless
lost necklace...and a timeless love.

Lilah and Suzanna
THE
Calhoun Women

**A special 2-in-1 edition containing
FOR THE LOVE OF LILAH and
SUZANNA'S SURRENDER**

Available at your favorite retail outlet.

SILHOUETTE®

Desire®

There is no sexier, stronger, more irresistible hero than Silhouette Desire's *Man of the Month.* And you'll find him steaming up the pages of a sensual and emotional love story written by the bestselling and most beloved authors in the genre.

Just look who's coming your way for the first half of 1998:

Man of the Month
only from

SILHOUETTE® *Desire®*

You can find us at your favorite retail outlet.

SUSAN MALLERY

Continues the twelve-book
series—36 HOURS—in
January 1998 with
Book Seven

THE RANCHER AND THE
RUNAWAY BRIDE

When Randi Howell fled the altar, she'd been running for her
life! And she'd kept on running—straight into the arms of
rugged rancher Brady Jones. She knew he had his suspicions,
but how could she tell him the truth about her identity? Then
again, if she ever wanted to approach the altar in earnest, how
could she not?

For Brady and Randi and *all* the residents of Grand Springs,
Colorado, the storm-induced blackout was just the beginning
of 36 Hours that changed *everything!* You won't want to
miss a single book.

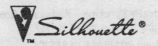

Available at your favorite retail outlet.

Look us up on-line at: http://www.romance.net

36HRS7

Welcome to the Towers!

In January
New York Times bestselling author

NORA ROBERTS

takes us to the fabulous Maine coast mansion
haunted by a generations-old secret and introduces
us to the fascinating family that lives there.

Mechanic Catherine "C.C." Calhoun and hotel magnate
Trenton St. James mix like axle grease and mineral
water—until they kiss. Efficient Amanda Calhoun finds
easygoing Sloan O'Riley insufferable—and irresistible.
And they all must race to solve the mystery
surrounding a priceless hidden emerald necklace.

Catherine and Amanda

THE Calhoun Women

**A special 2-in-1 edition containing
COURTING CATHERINE and A MAN FOR AMANDA.**

Look for the next installment of
THE CALHOUN WOMEN with Lilah and Suzanna's
stories, coming in March 1998.

Available at your favorite retail outlet.

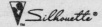

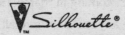